# SCREAMS PIERCED THE SMOKY AIR

Captain Shark led his bloodthirsty buccaneers through the dark corridors of the fortress, seeking revenge on the Spaniards who kept their shipmates captive. With his left hand he thrust the blazing torch into the Spanish captain's face. With his right toe he kicked the man betwixt wind and water. He hit him again as he went down, then he brought his rapier across and skewered a yelling soldier who was trying to brain him.

All about him his men were belting the guards back. Pistols snapped, and in the close confines of the stone corridors the choking smoke hung like filthy gray blankets.

"On, on!" bellowed Captain Shark.

They roared down into the bowels of the fortress, colliding head-on with a group of jailers who fell back, flabbergasted at the mad crowd of half-naked wretches, brandishing torches and swords and pistols, flooding toward them. The buccaneers were quick with them, and they pressed on . . .

# CAPTAIN SHARK

## By Pirate's Blood...

### Richard Silver

PINNACLE BOOKS • NEW YORK CITY

CAPTAIN SHARK: BY PIRATE'S BLOOD...

Copyright © 1975 by Richard Silver

An original Pinnacle Books edition, published for the first time anywhere.

ISBN: 0-523-00631-4

First Printing, May 1975

Printed in the United States of America

**PINNACLE BOOKS, INC.**
275 Madison Avenue
New York, N.Y. 10016

# By Pirate's Blood...

# CHAPTER ONE

Captain Shark's cutlass spattered brilliant splashes of blood as he wrenched its blade from the Spanish don's wrecked face.

"Up, you sea wolves!" he roared joyously, waving the reeking blade above his head. "Up! Slaughter every damned don aboard!"

"Aye, Cap'n!" his men bellowed, springing from their hiding places on the narrow, cramped deck of the sloop *Draco*. "Aye, Cap'n Shark! To hell with the Spanish dogs!"

Shark clamped the heavy cutlass between his strong yellow teeth and joined his men as they smashed their way up the ornately gilded quarter of the Spanish galleon. They pounded over the high bulwarks and down onto the decks in a mad welter of belching pistols and flashing blades. With their white-rimmed eyes blazing and their gap-toothed mouths yelling obscene promises, they struck mortal terror into the hearts of the Spaniards.

For a moment the Spanish stood, spellbound. Then a pistol cracked. Captain Shark's broad-brimmed black hat flew from his head like a wide-winged raven.

"My oath, Cap'n!" bellowed Tom Bowling. He

leveled his own piece. The priming took and the pistol cracked out. A richly attired Spanish grandee clutched his guts and toppled to the deck.

*"Corbleu!"* shouted Pierre Depoix, who had once been a marquis at the court of the Sun King. "We will feed the sharks' bellies this day!"

The little gaff-rigged, single-masted sloop *Draco* rocked in the long swells of the blue Caribbean Sea. The sun poured molten gold upon the sea and etched in fire the brilliant gilding and precious ornamentation of the galleon. Away to the north slender, graceful palm trees drooped in the heat; they seemed to grow from the seat itself, so narrow was the yellow spit of land whereon they had taken root. The eternal trade winds blew soughingly from the northeast. All in all, Captain Shark reckoned as his black-booted feet hit the deck and he wrenched the cutlass from his jaws, this was a delightful day for teaching the dons a few hard lessons.

Shark belted into the grandees. He didn't like them or their kind, and he had scars on his lean, whipcord-tough body to prove it. His cutlass flamed in that white-hot sunshine. His men roared into action at his back, but Shark was ever foremost in battle.

He took a grandee's rapier on his blade, twisted, slid, and drove the steel just far enough into the man's belly to do his business for him. With a twist he had his blade ready for the next Spanish devil.

Now the pistols had all been fired and it was cut and thrust. The sound of steel on steel rang and scraped all across the decks of the Spanisher. She was a fine large galleon, driven out of company of her escorts by the recent gale. She had appeared to Shark like the realization of a divine promise. She rode deeply in the water. The thought of that made

Shark's avaricious eyes gleam in anticipation as he fought.

"God's curse on ye for black-poxed heathen papists!" screeched John Fakenham. His tall, thin, grotesquely jointed body jerked into the fray. His lined face, parched and gray and unlike the suntanned faces of his fellow buccaneers, displayed a ferocious and fanatical religious zeal. Fakenham was older than most of the buccaneers, and had served as a lad in Oliver Cromwell's Ironsides. His Puritan ethic had been severely tested by the Inquisition. Now he shared his resolve to cleanse the seas of the murdering Spanish with Shark and the other Brethren of the Coast.

And the Spanish now realized they faced a dreaded band of men. They heard the yells of the buccaneers. They heard with horror the terrifying name.

*Captain Shark!*

They reeled back. Shark's men knew exactly what they were doing. There was nothing fancy in their fighting—save when circumstances dictated a fancy stroke and they didn't rush to haul down the arrogant red and gold flag of Spain, nor did they attempt to seize any particular part of the ship.

They went hunting dons.

The Spanish soldiers firing from the close-houses had to be dealt with first. The little round houses, cunningly looped for harquebus fire, always presented a problem. Situated at the break of the quarterdeck and the forecastle, sometimes even at the break of the poop, they commanded the decks and were difficult to assault. Captain Shark's men had developed their own particularly nasty way of getting at the soldiers within.

Here came Long Ned, his bronze face alight with

3

the frenzy of battle, a broad-bladed knife jammed between his lips. He was swinging a length of burning match in his left hand and clutching a canvas-wrapped bundle in his right.

"Up with you, Long Ned!" roared Shark.

"*Corbleu, mon capitaine!*" yelled Pierre Depoix. "Smoke them out so they may spit their bellies on my point!"

"There'll be plenty for you, Pierre! Watch that snake under your feet!"

Pierre Depoix laughed in his reckless Gascon way and leaped aside at Shark's yell. A Spaniard who had been shamming unconsciousness had tried to thrust his blade upward into the Gascon. But Depoix's long rapier slashed down in a crimson-flecked silver blur and the Spaniard shrieked—then he could shriek no more as the rapier sliced out his throat.

"My thanks, mon capitaine!"

"Up with Ned, now, Pierre! Tom, Harry—with me!"

The band rushed across the deck as Long Ned lit his evil concoction and looped it through the opening. Smoke gushed out from the round, cone-topped close-house. Soon the bolt screeched and the door bashed open. A Spanish soldier reeled out, coughing and choking, his face scarlet. He went down asprawl on the deck and the sea wolves howled on to their next encounter.

The buccaneers ran wild about the Spanisher as they chased the dons. Not until the last don was dead and the last Spanish seamen and soldiers had thrown down their arms and surrendered would Captain Shark and his men be satisfied.

As Shark had said before and as he bellowed

now: "Our quarrel is with the grandees! Give the poor devils of sailors a chance!"

"'Od's life, Cap'n!" said John Fakenham, his lined gray face grim and skull-like. "They be papists all, God rot 'em!"

"Aye, good John! And there are good papists and bad papists, as there are good Englishmen and bad Englishmen. I would I could cleanse the seas of the dons and let an honest sailorman breathe fresh life, stab me!"

"When the Lord's will is done, Cap'n!"

And John Fakenham, that tall and thin man of great religious conviction, went about his appointed business of exterminating the grandees of Spain.

Over the blue sea the horrible sounds drifted on the eternal trades. Gradually the clang of steel and the chopped-off screams, the grunting shrieks of mortal agony, faded and died. The Spanish galleon drifted in the sea, her canvas clewed up, her main topsail to the mast, rolling and yawing and uselessly idle. After a time the sounds of battle faded completely and only the tuneful bellow of a rollicking song from Barbados Ben lifted to show the Spaniard was any different from the ship she had been an hour before, when the big galleon had dropped insolently down onto Captain Shark's little sloop.

At first, while his men were hidden about his tiny command, Shark had spoken very humbly to the arrogant Spanish captain. But that had not saved him, and the Spaniard sent down an officer and a few men to turn over what might be found in this suspicious sloop. Then, when Shark had slammed his heavy cutlass into the don's face and hallooed his sea wolves into action, he revealed to the Spanish just what manner of horror they had unleashed upon themselves.

The Spanisher was called the *Doña Rosaria* and as Captain Shark made his way about her capacious gun deck, looked down the opened hatches onto the orlop, and had his first appraising look into the hold, she appeared to him to be a very great prize indeed. The Spanish had suffered a hundred years of raids and ship losses in the Caribbean and along the Spanish Main, and these days they tended to sail in convoys, heavily escorted. The pirate trade—although Shark was never a pirate—was becoming ever more risky. *Doña Rosaria* had been delivered up to Shark by the chance of a gale, and he was more than half inclined to favor John Fakenham's view that the storm was divinely inspired.

"However it be," he said to Simon de Rycke, his Flemish lieutenant, "someone up there smiled on us this day."

"Aye, Cap'n," said de Rycke in his accented English. "And the damned dons have felt the shadow of a frown."

They prowled with Long Ned, the boatswain, with Pierre Depoix, and with Patch to hold a lantern, from the gundeck up to the waist and so via the ladder—with a smoke-blackened close-house to bear eloquent testimony to the effectiveness of the evil compound used to smoke out the Spanish soldier—up on to the quarterdeck. That deck stretched wide and fair under the sun. The crucifix was displayed, the arms racks were broken open, and the Spanish blood was still rich and red upon the planks.

"Mother of God, entirely!" said Patrick Murphy, as he straightened up from the body of a buccaneer. Shark looked quickly at the corpse. It was John

Fairbanks, a fair-haired man from Cornwall. Now his lifeblood, too, stained the Spanish planks.

"I couldna save him, Cap'n. The ball tore out his guts—as ye can see."

Captain Shark nodded.

He hated to see his own men die thus. He knew that the Irish surgeon could have done nothing for John Fairbanks. Shark himself, through his knowledge of Arabic medical skill, was only too well aware that once a pistol ball ripped a man's guts out he stood no chance at all of surviving.

"Are there any more, Patrick?"

"Two have gone over the side, Cap'n, and young Andy Perkins has a slashed face."

"That'll make a man of him," said Samuel Percy, appearing from the waist of the ship. The red kerchief tied around his black hair and the gold ring in his ear gave him a rascally appearance that he thoroughly deserved. Captain Shark called Sam Percy his honest rascal. As first lieutenant he served well and faithfully, and Shark knew with a wonder that dimmed each day that Sam Percy would unhesitatingly give his own life for his captain's.

Now Percy bellowed his laughter. He had already found a flagon of wine and he upended it so that the bright drops splattered down his white shirt, a joyful surrogate for the grim blood drops already staining the garment.

"Faith, Sam Percy," said the surgeon, standing up and putting his hand to his back. "You'll drink the very waters of hell dry."

"An they taste as sweet as this, aye, sawbones, aye!"

"Is there aught of interest forward, Sam?" Shark knew that Percy would know exactly what he meant.

7

Percy took the flagon from his lips for a moment, just long enough to bellow: "Nothing, Cap'n! Gewgaws and Spanish sailors' trash. It's all here, in the staterooms, I'll wager!"

They all laughed at this.

Shark maintained a strict and ruthless discipline at sea, in battle, during maneuvers. But once the fighting was done and the buccaneers could get down to the pleasurable task of sorting through the loot, every man had a right to speak his mind. Now they went aft through the ornately carved doors and into the cabins beneath the poop.

"She lies low in the water, mon capitaine," said Pierre Depoix with a huge smile, his black mustaches lifting in glee. "*Corbleu*! How they will fight for her treasures when we take her into Port Royal!"

"We might do better to patronize your fellows, and make for the Tortugas," said Sam Percy. "The old ways are dying along the Spanish Main."

"Wherever we take her we'll make such a fortune—" began Captain Shark as he stepped into the great aft cabin with its serried rank of stern windows. He stopped speaking. He stopped dead in his tracks so that Percy bumped into his broad, cambric-shirted back, and Depoix bumped into Percy.

Captain Shark stood there on the threshold of that luxurious stateroom. He stood tall and limber, wide-shouldered, his hands on his hips and the heavy bloodied cutlass dangling by its swordknot from his wrist. A full-lipped smile curved his mouth. He threw back his head so that his shoulder-length brown hair rippled. And he laughed. The long tanned line of his throat bubbled with that laughter. The others crowded past and halted and then

8

burst into reciprocal laughter, so that the tears flowed from their rascally eyes.

"By thunder!" roared Samuel Percy, that honest rascal. "Wenches! All laced and powdered and perfumed and lined up for us. By God, lads! It's a sight for sore eyes, God's truth on't!"

"Women bring evil and God's wrath upon the evil doer!" intoned John Fakenham.

"*Parbleu*! God's wrath has touched me thrice already and I look forward with horror to the next time!" Pierre Depoix swaggered into the cabin and swept his feathered hat off his curly hair and across his body in a deep bow. "Mesdemoiselles! I am at your service."

The buccaneers rushed eagerly into the cabin, bellowing their delight at the Gascon's jest. As Shark's merry eyes surveyed the scene, he stopped laughing. He looked at the five girls and and their elderly companion and chaperon. He marked them all as high-spirited and arrogant, Spanish to the core. The girl in the center was slender and narrow-waisted, and her small high breasts were confined in an elaborate bodice. Her creamy complexion was ablaze with the passions of horror and pride. He saw that she held her right hand behind the skirts of her emerald green gown.

"Hold, Pierre!" bellowed Shark.

The Gascon jumped at the crisp bark of command in his captain's voice, and Shark leaped forward. He reached the girl even as she whipped the little pistol up. The thing exploded almost by his ear so that the world rang with the fizz and bang of exploding gunpowder, but he had caught her wrist and directed the ball aloft. It cracked into the decking overhead. She wrestled with him for a space, her eyes blazing, her slender form struggling and writhing.

9

Shark held her as he would a fractious filly, too young yet for the rein or harness.

At last she quieted. She remained perfectly still except for the creamy expanse of her bosom above the bodice, which moved betrayingly. Her cheeks were flushed.

"By the gout-ridden foot of Saint Bartholomew!" Sam Percy tumbled the nearest girl to the deck, kicking her hands away, and other buccaneers similarly investigated the other girls.

There were no more pistols.

"For me, señorita, or yourself?"

Shark's lean face, hard with the years of toil and struggle, bore down on the girl. His brown eyes bored hypnotically into her black eyes. She lowered her gaze. His face, his voice, his eyes! They cowed her. And she, the daughter of a grandee of Spain! It was intolerable. Señorita Isabella Urraca Castileja de la Cuerva had lived in fear of this long journey from Spain to the New World and back again. Even when she had trodden the decks of this fine galleon, the *Doña Rosaria*, the dread had not left her. The seas swarmed with pirates. Their names were accursed in the sight of God. And now—now she had fallen into the clutches of the arch-scoundrel, the black, the infamous, the monstrous, the villainous Captain Sebastian Shark!

Yet—yet she could not rightly say if she had intended the pistol ball for this monster or for herself.

She struggled to find her voice, to compose herself, to stand defiantly before the rough hands and lecherous eyes of these pirates. She had no illusions about what would follow.

In a clear voice Isabella Urraca said: "You may do what the devil commands you to do, Captain

10

Shark, and you will answer for your crimes at the bar of heaven—"

"God's tooth! The wench speaks passable English!" exclaimed Sam Percy. He was busily ripping the jewels from the gown of the girl he had tripped and throwing them into a spread-open kerchief on the deck.

"English!" cried Isabella Castileja in a voice of scorn and loathing. "I speak your foul dog's tongue, to my shame!"

"A spritely wench," observed Tom Bowling, looking up from the open chest whose iron bands had been savagely ripped off. He lifted out a gilt-on-silver cup and laughed. "Give me gold and a drop o' rum anyday, Cap'n—and you can keep all the wenches in Christendom for me!"

"But assuredly, mon ami Tom," said Pierre Depoix as the buccaneers set about the cabin, "you do not understan' the finer t'ings of life. . ."

"What!" bellowed Tom Bowling. "What's finer than a bracer o' rum and a sack o' ducats, eh, Pierre? Answer me that, if'n you can!"

"Ducats, is it, Tom!" cat-called Long Ned as he rummaged. "Pieces o' eight not good enough for you, eh, my finicky lad?"

As the rummaging and the badinage went on, the Spanish ladies stood together, white-faced, staring, bosoms heaving, filled with the most dreadful imaginings of their eventual fate. Isabella Castileja tried to remain calm, tried to calm the fears of her compatriots; but the fierce aspect of these sea rovers, the glint of gold rings in their ears, the scarlet kerchiefs wound about their hair, the clatter of their weapons as they moved, the jovial promising gleam of their eyes—all, all drove a deep shuddering terror deep into her heart.

11

Everything taken from the Spaniard would be shared. Shark had built up a tightly knit crew and each man knew what he must do under the Articles. There would be no holdouts. These men were, in turth, the best of the Brotherhood of the Coast. They were called pirates by the Spanish, their victims. On occasion a trifle of piracy could be proved against them, and on occasion the carefully drawn-up Articles were contravened. Captain Shark knew he trod a tightrope.

"The poor devils of Spanish are ready to cast off, Cap'n," Samuel Percy called through the door, his honest, cheerful face alight with the mischief and love of life that so endeared him to Captain Shark. "You might care to say a few words of prayer over their heathen carcasses."

Isabella heard this and misunderstood and could not prevent herself from letting out a sharp, stifled shriek of dismay and horror. Captain Shark turned to her with a frown on his lean devil's face, a frown which turned instantly to a gallant smile. He bowed elegantly.

"You misunderstand, my lady. We have no quarrel with the poor devils of seamen you employ about your stinking ships, whom you whip and jerk and starve. They will be set free in a boat. Land and a safe anchorage is not far."

She lifted her chin at him so that her small high breasts jutted arrogantly. Her face flamed with two spots of crimson on each smooth cheek.

"Indeed, my lady," said Shark. "You do us an injustice."

Laughing, he went up on deck. The seamen and those few soldiers that remained were huddled in the ship's boats. Shark leaned over the rail, glaring down, and the faces in the boats below stared up, brown with sun and wind. The thought occurred to him that with a single word he might order all these miserable men killed. Many a buccaneer would have given that order—aye, and joyed in the giving and the execution of it. But that was not Sebastian Shark's way. Since he had taken the name Shark, he had grown accustomed to thinking of himself as Captain Sebastian Shark. The name suited him passing well.

"Cast off!"

The boats were set adrift and soon their oars splashed overside and began pulling the boats toward the bending forms of the palms upon the dazzling horizon. Shark wiped his forehead. The Caribbean was like a furnace, cooking a man's blood to a red pudding.

"Here be your hat, Cap'n," said Tom Bowling. Tom was as near a manservant as one buccaneer might expect of another. Whatever he called himself, Tom Bowling knew that it was his place to look out for and care for Captain Shark.

"Thankee, Tom." Shark put his finger through the pistol-ball hole. "I'll not forget that whiz-bang in a hurry."

"*Sail ho!*"

The cry echoed about the ship and the buccaneers rushed to the rail. Some climbed halfway up the ratlines. Shark would not be hurried. Whatever ship might be out there she would be friend or enemy. If friend, a merry carousing night lay ahead. If enemy—and there and then Shark's cunning and devious mind surveyed all the many possibilities in the situation. H'mm. There might be more pickings to add to *Dona Rosaria*. . .

"Secure the women, Pierre!" he yelled as the first necessary preliminary to what might follow.

13

Then he sauntered to the rail and sprang up into the shrouds, climbing a few of the ratlines until he could espy fairly the pile of yellow-brown canvas hurling on across the blue sea. He smiled, his wide mobile mouth curving in a grimace of amused regret and distaste. He had recognized the cut of that foretopsail. It was unmistakable, and even as he recognized it a hoarse voice bellowed above his head.

"Ahoy, there! She's *Black Lace*! Cap'n Hagger's *Black Lace*!"

"Goddamn his eyes!" Sam Percy slapped a hand to his cutlass hilt. "He's no friend of ours!"

"Aye, Sam. But he's no Spanisher, either."

"If ever a black dog deserved to be called a pirate, Bloody Fist Hagger does."

"And he'll be licking his lips now and counting over the pieces of eight he thinks already in his hand when he takes *Doña Rosaria*." Captain Shark roared the jest out and his cutthroat crew bellowed their enjoyment. "He's cracking on all sail to board and take this ship. An unwelcome surprise awaits the bastard—that's for sure!"

"A pox on Capitaine Hagger," said Pierre Depoix, coming up on deck and ruffling the lace rabato at his throat. "The ladies are stowed below, mon capitaine. I'll wager that dog Hagger would give much for them and their ransoms."

*Black Lace* sped over the sea, taking the wind, all her canvas drawing. She was pierced for eleven guns on each side of the gun deck, with a further battery on her quarterdeck and forecastle. Shark's little sloop *Draco* would have stood no chance against *Black Lace*. But *Draco* was hidden behind the tall glistening side of *Doña Rosaria*, and it was quite clear Captain Hagger thought he was bearing up for

14

a fat and juicy prize. His disappointment and the black evil of his anger would serve a pretty sauce to the rapseallion crew of Captain Shark's *Draco*, to be sure.

Mind you, it occurred to Captain Shark, as he watched the oncoming ship coursing over the sunflecked sea, that there were tales of the deeds of Captain Sebastian Shark among the islands and along the Spanish Main, and this one would not suit ill among such company. He had grown in stature since achieving his first command, and taking the title Captain. Not for Sebastian the sure onward progress of naval ranks, the influence and the money, the ship commands, and the ears of powerful friends at home and at court. For young Sebastian there had been a hard-working youth among the boatmen of his native West Country town. Then he was captured by the corsairs out of Barbary, and enslaved. He suffered the horrors of the heathen galley benches; then he was delivered and began a new life that had, in the sure course of the doom he felt laid upon him by a Divinity he could not begin to understand, come to a shocking end. Now he had a fresh new life as a buccaneer and—sometime—pirate here in the Caribbean.

He shook the gray ghost memories from him—and he not yet thirty years of age!—and went aft to see what manner of rapiers the dons had left for his inspection and choice.

The bloodied cutlass could be left for Tom Bowling to clean to a bright sparkle with spittle and brick dust. The cutlass was the weapon for the smash and bash of boarding and the heavy work of piracy; Shark's own rapier had swung at his side throughout the attack. Had the need arisen, he would have drawn it like the flicker of a serpent's tongue and so fallen to, for Captain Shark was mightily skilled at fence with the rapier.

He felt the slow surge of the ship beneath his booted feet, and he frowned.

Instead of making his way aft he shouted to Long Ned, and to Patch to bring his lantern, and went clattering down the hatchway ladder. The gundeck stretched about him, but he ignored that and the glistening shadowed bulks of the twin rows of the Spanish mediocanon (they were brass guns, what the English called demicannon, and they fired shot of approximately thirty-two pounds; if necessary, Shark would fire them at Bloody Fist Hagger, by God!). As he went down to the hold, with the exaggerated shadows of Patch's lantern hurrying about him, he wondered if he would even be vouchsafed enough time to draw the tampions.

"By God!" yelled Long Ned. "Here, Patch, throw your light here, damn you for a one-eyed lubber."

The light revealed the water seeping between the close-packed bundles, and slopping against the hogsheads and the barrels. The water shone with multicolored whirls in the light, shimmering rainbowlike with grease and oil. Shark nodded with savage amusement.

"The damned dons have beaten us to their own ship, Ned!"

"The devils stove in the bottom—somewhere— before they were brought out. But where?" The light danced crazily in the confined spaces between bales and barrels.

Shark felt the ship move in the sea. He knew.

"It matters not where. She's going down. We'll never save her now!" Shark sprang back to the deck, bellowing, filled with fury. "She's sinking, God rot the dons! Back to *Draco* before she takes us with her to hell!"

## CHAPTER TWO

A ship of the build of *Doña Rosaria*—broad, comfortable, with high sides, and towering quarterdeck and poop—would take some time to sink. There would be time enough for Shark's desperadoes to carry off a wonderful selection of treasures from the doomed vessel. Like ants the buccaneers jumped from ship to sloop, their arms loaded with plunder, then jumped back again for more. Shark looked over the side.

The sea slopped against the wales of the ship. He estimated times and functions and capacities. Once the water reached the lowest tier of gunports—well, the sea would pour into the ship and she would go down like a plummet.

"Pierre! Take the women aboard."

"With the greatest of pleasures, mon capitaine." The Gascon's plumed hat swept off in an elaborate bow and his bright eyes twinkled with mischief as he invited the ladies to step down into the little *Draco*.

For all his airs and gallantries, Pierre Depoix kept his hand near the butt of his pistol. Shark knew he would not hesitate to pistol even so fine and fair a

17

lady as the leader of these Spanish señoritas if she so deserved.

Shark stroked his long, curling mustaches as he watched the women leave the stricken galleon. The dark-eyed one who had tried to pistol him—or herself—was clearly a lady of birth and position. But the leader was the one for whom Pierre reserved admiring glances. She stepped out haughtily, supported by the old confidante, and by the dark-eyed one, who gave a helping hand under the leader's elbow.

"She is one ready for the plucking," observed Pierre. He twisted his mustache in a gesture vastly different from Shark's. "*Corbleu*! Is her ransom worth the deprivation?"

"There could be a mystery here, Pierre, and one well worth solving."

"Oui! I agree. I suppose that those who tried to fight us were their husbands and lovers, and so, consequently. . ." Here Pierre gave a Gallic shrug and glanced around the deck. The bloody corpses of the Spaniards lay there still, and now no one was going to waste time heaving them overboard. They would all go down to the sharks with the ship. The women hurried past, their mantillas shielding their faces as they turned their heads from the sight.

One girl let rip with a shriek that, in other circumstances, would have wrung Shark's heartstrings. As it was he bellowed and Tom Bowling hustled up and tore the weeping girl from the dead body of her father. Shark watched, his face like stone.

"*Ma foix*! This mystery, mon capitaine—five girls and a confidante and. . ." Pierre shrugged again. They stood to watch as the girls were hustled aboard *Draco* and sent below.

18

"Bloody Fist Hagger's mighty close, Cap'n!" yelled Sam Percy.

Shark had already calculated the approximate times.

"*Doña Rosaria* will go just as he fetches up with her, Sam."

Sam Percy, that honest rascal, bellowed his delight at this.

Although Shark remained furious with himself for allowing the dons to sink their ship, he had already accepted it. The ship was going. The bucaneers would take what they could loot and let her go. There would be other ships, despite the fact that the Spanish kept more and more to armed convoys and their shipping became scarcer every year.

"Keep moving there." Shark bustled his men along. They were in this buccaneering business for a variety of reasons. The most important reason now was to secure what loot they could to tide them over until the next pickings came along. Times were harder than they had been in the old days, when the buccaneers were just beginning to prove that there were other men alive in the New World besides the arrogant bastards from New Spain.

Nowadays a buccaneer had to be lighter of foot and smarter of mind than ever before. This great puffing, panting devil of a pirate, Bloody Fist Hagger, now, whose ship was coming up fast, why, he was one of your old-time pirates, all blood and murder and sin. Though he'd not gone with Henry Morgan to the sack of Panama, as Shark had done, because he'd drawn back out of caution. Caution had no business in the inventory of a buccaneer, God and the devil knew!

*Black Lace* in this kind of sea could not hope to

19

match *Draco* for speed, but if the wave height should increase, the smashing bulk of *Black Lace* and her cloud of canvas would soon overtop *Draco*. Knowing this, Shark could wait insolently until the last moment before giving his orders to get the sloop under way. All the loose loot had been gathered in and Long Ned and a party had even broken open a few choice items from below. Shark had cast a covetous eye upon the galleon's guns, for their bronze—commonly called brass—would ensure them a value; but with the galleon sinking, and with a pirate ship looming up with the wind, there was just no time for the delicate business of bringing the guns aboard.

Shark eyed *Black Lace*.

She was a fine vessel, of that there was no doubt. One day, perhaps, Shark might care to invest his fortunes in such a craft. As of now, this little single-masted sloop, called *Draco* as he called most of his commands *Draco*, suited him admirably.

"All clear!" bellowed Long Ned, at last, appearing at the rail and waving a wine bottle over his head. "All clear, Cap'n—an' she's agoing!"

"Cast off," said Shark in his usual calm and melodious voice. "Up with the canvas. Take her out finely, Ben," he said to Barbados Ben at the tiller.

That squat ruffian chuckled and ducked his head so that his black ringlets danced and the gold ring in his ear glittered in the brilliant Caribbean sunshine.

"Aye, Cap'n. We'll show Bloody Fist Hagger our arse, and he knows what I'd like to do to him."

*Draco* danced across the water and quickly settled down to that long sure rhythm of movement that sprang from a sweetly raked hull and a goodly area of canvas. Shark stood with his booted feet

20

apart and stared back at the sinking bulk of *Doña Rosaria* and at the growing pile of canvas from *Black Lace*, as Hagger's ship clawed around the wreck.

"Faith!" said Patrick Murphy, his hand shading his eyes. "He'll not be wanting fuel to stoke his anger!"

"Badcess to him," grunted Simon de Rycke. The Fleming's active body looked fine-drawn and ready to spring.

Shark understood the temper of his men. He lifted his voice, an instrument of brutal power or of gentle and winning melody, whichever he chose it to be.

"Harkee, men! Bloody Fist Hagger has nigh on three times as many men as we are. And he has guns that can blow us out of the water before we could get in to board—aye, and after that we'd still take the bastard!"

"Aye, Cap'n!" they roared.

"But, today, we sail away." He gestured to where *Black Lace* had regained her former course and, with all her canvas pulling, came haring along with a bone betwixt her teeth. "Tomorrow—ah!"

They roared back at him; but he could sense their desperate desire to have a smack at Bloody Fist Hagger. Captain Shark had not lived so long without being able to cast up the accounts in Destiny's locker of chances. He could take *Black Lace*. Oh, yes, he could stand to her punishment and run in and board her, and his sea wolves would tear the throats out of Hagger's bastards. But he'd lose men, good men, men who were precious to him—for they would follow him into the scarlet-fanged black jaws of hell itself. They were men who were seamen and fighters, men who knew how to handle a ship, men who could not be bought cheaply. Desperadoes all, they were a choice crew.

No, decided Sebastian, soberly. No, the chances of losing half his crew just to spite Bloody Fist Hagger were not acceptable.

The Captain had spoken and his crew would obey.

They watched from the bulwarks as *Draco* picked up speed, foaming along in fine style. *Black Lace* pulled away from the widening pool where *Doña Rosaria* plunged in her last agony. She went down stern first and for a long instant her bowsprit speared into the bright air. Then, with a groaning sigh audible clearly over the sea, she sank and the bowsprit vanished into the white boil.

"She's gone."

Samuel Percy, halfway up the ratlines, waved his hat at *Black Lace* and laughed despite the loss of the prize. "And may you go down to perdition likewise, Bloody Fist!" he roared. It was easy come, easy go for the crew of *Draco*.

Shark glanced up at his first lieutenant. What a rascal Sam Percy was! He could bash an indolent crew into men fitter to man a King's ship than to sail a crafty buccaneer. His stalwart athletic form outlined against the brilliant pallor of the sky summed up for Captain Shark almost all the pleasures to be had from the buccaneering life.

Aboard *Black Lace* Bloody Fist Hagger was not pleased, and his squat frame, in black taffetas relieved only by a foppish display of sumptuous lace, convulsed in fury. He roared obscenely, raving at Captain Shark, that damned lily-livered pansy-fingered bastard who called himself a buccaneer.

A puff of white broke from the bows of *Black Lace*.

22

"He doesn't share the joke," observed Shark, laughing gently.

"But the jest is on him, Cap'n," said Sam Percy, and he laughed, his bright face alight with the rascality and the mischief that so endeared him to Captain Shark.

Hagger's intemperate order to fire a last despairing shot at *Draco* had brought him nothing in return—or so Bloody Fist Hagger must then have thought.

No one aboard *Draco* saw where the shot went. No one bothered to check. They heard its rustling, whistling passage overhead, and Shark was congratulating himself that no vital spar or sheet had been struck when he saw Sam Percy fall from the ratlines.

Sam fell with a headlong smash to the deck. Shark led the rush to him. He bent over the fallen body of his friend and first lieutenant.

There was not a mark on Samuel Percy, but his face was blue, and he was dead.

Stone dead.

"By God!" said Patrick Murphy, the surgeon. "I've seen that afore, boys. It's the passage of the shot, d'ye see—"

"Aye, Patrick, we see," said Captain Shark. He spoke in a voice that turned them all mute.

Tenderly, Shark lifted the unmarked body of Sameul Percy. He turned to face his crew, holding the corpse in his arms.

"We will make Sam ready for burial, and we will bury him, with all due formality."

Pierre Depoix did not lift his eyes to look at his captain, as he said: "We will turn back and punish this foul Hagger—?"

"No," said Shark. His mind had been made up.

23

This would not alter that. "No. We do as we planned. Tomorrow—tomorrow Bloody Fist Hagger will wish he had not been born."

They all knew Sebastian Shark did not mean the tomorrow that would begin on the following day; he was talking of a future time when just retribution would overtake Bloody Fist Hagger.

"In due time," whispered Sebastian Shark. "In due time."

# CHAPTER THREE

It was said of Captain Shark by his friends that he was by far too finicky in his dealings with his enemies. It was said of him by his enemies—but, then, what Sebastian Shark's enemies had to say of him would have filled thrice over one of those great chained leather-bound bibles, and still there would have been more. Suffice it to say that any man who knew Sebastian Shark even slightly would never say a jot or tittle that might put the Captain out of countenance in matters of honor, or seafaring, or the proper treatment of ladies, or the proper treatment of Spanish dons.

The five ladies with their chaperon were brought out on deck later that day, after the mournful business of committing Samuel Percy's body to the deeps had been carried out with due solemnity. Shark valued friends. He did not make friends easily and never went out of his way to cultivate anyone——except, perhaps ironically, some Spanish grandee he was fattening up for the kill.

Now he stood at his ease regarding the six females.

The confidante appeared to him to be a typical

example of her breed; over-refined, cantankerous, querulous, supremely zealous in guarding the young ladies committed to her care. Her lean and yet jowly face—for the climate and the food could do wondrous things to a woman's face in the West Indies—glowered at the buccaneer captain. He made a polite bow to her and turned his attention to the younger ladies.

He deliberately did not look at Isabella. She seemed to him to partake of a species of forbidden fruit, delicious but with a bitterness at the core, and he wanted no part of her.

The acknowledged leader, he knew, for Isabella had once spoken her name, was the Duchess Marfisa Esmerelda de Ariza y Medelina. She stood upon the deck of Captain Shark's vessel now in a sullen and haughty silence. Her cheek betrayed more pallor than was usual, even for a great lady whose desire would be always to keep her face shielded from the rays of the sun. Her ornate gown of lace and silk showed rips and tears, and no doubt a few of Shark's men might answer for that, had they wished.

Shark looked at the Duchess Marfisa for a long moment and then regarded the remaining three girls. All wore fine and fancy gowns with much lace, and great and toppling mantillas; all wore white gloves, and all had their faces well-powdered. Shark smiled. He bent closer.

"My lady," he said to Isabella. "As you are the only one to speak our abominable English tongue, I ask you to request these three ladies to remove their—gloves."

Isabella caught her breath at the ironical pause.

Shark's smile remained aloof, ironical. He would not give this girl the satisfaction of knowing he spoke Spanish—the pure Castilian taught him by poor Don Jaime so long ago, and the Catalán and the waterfront argot he had picked up later—and, anyway, it pleased him to employ her as an interpreter. She did not lift her eyes as she said:

"For what reason do you thus shame us?"

"I! Shame you? By asking these three—ladies—to remove their gloves? You have misjudged me once before. You do so again."

She remained silent.

This was no sort of game for a man of Shark's sensibilities. He spoke, and the hint of steel in his voice sent Isabella's head back and brought gasps from the Spanish ladies who could not understand what he said in so savage a fashion.

"Tell them to remove their gloves, my lady, or my men will strip them away for them!"

Isabella, seeing the game played out, did as she was bid.

The three pairs of white gloves fell to the deck.

Shark seized the hand of the nearest girl and lifted it high. It was broad and blunt-fingered, red with toil, and yet it was not the hand of a common serving wench. It betrayed that these three were not ladies. Ladies' maids, no doubt.

"You beast!" flamed Isabella. "You would—you would—"

"I would, indeed, my lady."

She subsided.

"*Corbleu!*" said Pierre Depoix. "I see!"

"Aye," said Shark. "And, in God's truth, Pierre, one must do these poor creatures honor, for all they are Spanish to the core."

No pity for the girls entered Shark's heart. He felt for them only the same sorrow he felt for all humanity. He knew well enough that had they been two English ladies who had dressed up their per-

27

sonal maids, placed white gloves on their hands, and powdered their faces, he would have felt a hot pride, a great joy and a sweet compassion. But, save for the memory of Don Jaime, Sebastian Shark could harbor no human thoughts whatsoever regarding anything Spanish.

Save, of course, their ships, their rapiers, and their gold.

"What's to do, then, Cap'n?"

Simon de Rycke looked with a hard glance upon his captain, and then at the three maids, who shrank back, looking ridiculous in their borrowed finery. "They be nothing better than doxies, I'll be bound."

"I think not, Simon. God knows we have cause enough to hate all things Spanish. But—" Shark bestowed on the three maids so fierce and mean a glance they let out squeals of fear and hid their faces in their naked hands.

"You would not dishonor us, in dishonoring these poor girls, Captain Shark?"

Isabella forced the loathed name through stiff lips. She had keyed herself up to the horror she thought bound to follow on capture by a devilish raping pirate. But the three maids. . . As for Marfisa, the Duchess de Ariza, she could look out for herself.

"I would dishonor Spain, were that not a task beyond man's endeavor, for Spain has dishonored herself in the sight of God and the world long since."

"You—"

"Aye, my lady! Call me what you will. It will be nothing to what I have been called already by your Spanish dogs."

*Ma foi, mon capitaine*! The problem yet remains."

28

"Yes, Pierre. Let the ladies and their maids be taken below and properly cared for. The confidante, too. I will not tolerate any man's interference with them."

Isabella laughed shrilly at this. She held her clenched hands to her belly. Her fears seemed to have congested into a knot there. "You would not tolerate interference, you English swine, because you would take the interference all for yourself!"

"Mam'selle!" exclaimed Pierre Depoix, highly offended. He stared at Isabella. "You do not know Capitaine Shark! In Tortuga, where any girl is a wanton, it seems, Capitaine Cuda himself sought to take a girl by force. She was a common doxy, but she wanted nothing of Capitaine Cuda, my oath! Sebastian warned this Cuda, this black dog. He said: 'You touch that girl, and I will pistol you!'"

"Aye!" said Simon de Rycke. "And the fool laughed and seized the girl and the cap'n put a ball through his brains!"

Isabella shuddered.

The captain looked away from her.

He understood perfectly what he was doing, and took no joy from that. There was a mystery here, as Pierre had said, and even if that mystery was a little one, say a willful girl with all the nobility of a Spanish duchess running from an unwanted suitor or an arranged marriage, he must still discover all there was to know. By asking a few careless questions, by implying threats, by keeping these girls poised to a pitch of terror, he would eventually uncover the mystery. The only excuse he could offer for this despicable conduct was that they were Spanish. But then, that that was no excuse. That was the whole reason.

They went below in a bustle, and later he would

hale them on deck again, and ask a few more
questions, and his men would look at them and lick
their lips, and down below again they could go.
Soon they would be happy to tell him all he
wanted to know, and this without anyone's laying a
finger on them.

To say that Captain Sebastian Shark was an
inhuman man was, of course, merely to state what
seemed the obvious truth to his enemies. The crew
of *Draco* knew firmly the difference. They had
many times been given ample proof of the warmth
and humanity of the captain.

"New Providence, I think," he said to Simon de
Rycke. Shark spoke briskly.

"Aye aye, Cap'n," said the Fleming, without
thought to question the order. Port Royal, Tortuga,
New Providence, and a host of lesser pirate haunts
lay waiting for them. They would carouse and have
themselves a good time and sell their plunder and,
faith, when all was spent, why, it would be to sea
again!

A short life and a merry one, they said, in the
sweet trade.

*Draco* sailed to the northwest on the starboard
tack, with Shark charting a careful course to run
clear of Hispaniola's western coastline and to sail
on through the Windward Passage, a neatly tricky
piece of navigation. And Shark was just as firmly
sure of his own personal life's course. Buccaneering
was not for him a short life and a merry one. Faith!
Merry it would be, surely; but short—no. He might
be only a miserable boatboy hauled from the stews
by chance to the command of a vessel, but his plans
envisioned the amassing of a sizeable fortune. Then
he would return to England where, if all went well,
he could take up the life of a gentleman. He could

do it. He knew well enough the mysteries of swapping identities. His disguises were legion. After he had dealt with those mercenary swine who had sold him to the Barbary corsairs such memories, those!—he would settle down on a broad estate in the West Country and become the gentleman of gentlemen, the sine qua non, and to hell with pirating and the sea!

And that small matter of a murder charge hanging over his head—until he had proved his innocence there could be no safe return. He had no wish to go back to England, even in a safe disguise, if he was not absolutely satisfied that no one would stumble upon him as an unhanged murderer!

With the trades seeming never to end their eternal blowing—although a gale could whip up at any time and blow with furious energy from the west or southwest—*Draco*'s slim stem was turned northwest again with Cape Maysi falling away to leeward. Shark knew the Bahama Islands well, and he knew many a cay where he might lie up, or careen, or merely take on wood and water. Most of the tiny, scattered islands were deserted, and their coral structure lay low in the sea. Except for Andros, where there was a natural stream, fresh water was had by means of wells. Shark felt that peculiar sense of peacefulness fall upon him as his vessel bore onward through the blue waters, with the flash and glitter of the sun off the waves, and the steady breeze, and the tall sky with its fleecy clouds far above. By God! This was the life for a bold buccaneer!

His interest in his female captives stirred him to attempt to uncover their secret—purely because a secret, he felt convinced, existed. What the secret was did not move him overmuch, although Pierre

31

Depoix was agog to uncover it.

Shark had discovered by listening to the girls' conversations that the dark-eyed Isabella Urraca Castileja de la Cuerva was the niece of Don Garcia, who was a hidalgo of great wealth, although his powers were limited to those his sovereign cared to enturst him with. The grandees of Spain had fallen into a sad decay, and had grown corrupt and vicious in these later days.

The mystery did not, Shark considered, lie with her.

He overhead Isabella talking to the still haughty Duchess Marfisa, and he stood for a space leaning gently to the roll and surge of his vessel as the girls talked.

"The man is a beast, a *ladrón*, a *corsario luterano*, Isabella! How can you say he treats us well?"

"I did not say he treats us well, Marfisa."

Shark noted Isabella's use of the Duchess's Christian name.

"If he comes near me I will stick him with my dagger!"

Shark smiled.

"I would have shot him," said Isabella, her dark eyes very fierce. "The poor fool thought I meant to kill myself. He does not understand us Spanish ladies, I think."

"And yet, Isabella, he very soon understood the maids were not ladies."

"That! Poof! The man is a clod, a murderer, a rapist!"

"Yes. And I know where my honor leads me."

Shark moved away. He did not savor this eavesdropping; and the girls were no nearer explaining the mystery in this futile and pitiful talk. He treated them all with the exquisite courtesy of which he was a master.

The Duchess Marfisa said to Isabella: "If my cousin, Don Pedro, knows his business, as I think he does, he will have a hundred ships scouring the seas for me!"

"Then, Marfisa, I pray Our Gracious Virgin he finds us before this Shark has his will of us."

As she spoke, Isabella pressed her clenched fists into her belly, low, where all her fears congested and made her feel weak and sick.

This Captain Shark! In Doña Isabella's eyes his trouble was not that he was a despised and hated Englishman, but that he was a man.

The Duchess Marfisa's cousin, Don Pedro, was engaged in the most entertaining of pursuits. As governor of San Isidro he carried under his hand the power of the king, and nothing gave him more pleasure in the exercise of that power than indulging his passion for letting the blood of heretics.

Four of these condemned creatures hung before him now, a Dutchman, two Englishmen, and a Dane. They had shrieked until they had ripped their throats hoarse. The brilliant West Indian sunshine could not penetrate into the dank depths of the cellars and holes and dungeons beneath this old castle that perched atop a rock at the harbor entrance. Once inside the landlocked harbor of San Isidro, Don Pedro boasted, any ship of Spain was perfectly safe. The same could not be said for a ship of Spain upon the Caribbean.

"Tighten another turn, Lorenzo," said Don Pedro. His elegantly affected speech slurred, thickened by the exciting spectacle of men being torn limb from limb, of men being flayed so their skins might be blown up and exhibited as bladders, the surrogate of living bodies.

Lorenzo turned the iron-spoked wheel and the

wretched man upon the rack shrieked once more, then shuddered with the sweat starting from him, and fell limply in a swoon that carried him to the very portals of death.

Don Pedro was a fat jowly man, ornately attired in pale lavender with much fine Flemish lace. He wore costly silks, ribbons, and bows, and fine gold chains strung about his corpulent person. His boots were polished into mirrors, and their fine leather gave his fat feet no discomfort, for he walked as seldom as possible. He still knew how to handle a rapier, and the weapon that swung at his side was no mere ornament.

Lorenzo grunted. "He is going, my lord."

"Let the *ladron* go, Lorenzo. He has served my purpose."

"Yes, my son," came the funereal voice of Father Jacinto. "But he dies unrepentant, a heretic still, condemned to burn forever in the fires of hell."

Father Jacinto, wearing a black cowl, black robes with scarlet linings, and wooden sandals, and with a great ebony cross swinging at his waist, presented a ghoulish figure in the flickering torchlight. The dungeon seemed a fit place for such as he. His gaunt face, deeply lined, revealed the soul of the flagellant. His burning eyes regarded the hideously distorted wretches hung upon the appliances of torture with the hungry greed of a man to whom pain and punishment were true offerings in the service of his God.

"Let them burn, Father, say I!"

"You run dangerously close upon the reefs of blasphemy, my son!"

The harsh words made Don Pedro's face jerk up with a look that would have frightened any of those who served his devious purposes with such dark skill. But Father Jacinto could not be moved by such petty displays of arrogant power. He knew where the power lay, in this sunburned island of San Isidro as in the sun-parched lands of Spain. Mother Church held the final, unalterable, absolute power, and no one dared forget it, including highborn hidalgos with direct powers from the king, His Most Catholic Majesty, Charles the Second. Yes, the king was an epileptic, and, yes, he was weak and corrupt; but he was guided by men like Father Jacinto, and therefore the priest did not overestimate the king's power.

The French king, Louis the Fourteenth—whom his dazzled subjects idolatrously called The Sun King—sought to tear huge chunks of Spanish dominions away, and the Austrian faction at court sought to claim for themselves powers they imagined themselves heirs to. To be Spanish at this time, considered Father Jacinto, laid heavy burdens upon a man of inner strength and intellect and religious convictions.

These four *demonios* before him now—they were the scum of the seas and deserved to burn in hellfire as the governor had said; but Father Jacinto passionately wished for them to see the light of the True Way. If he could force them to recant their heresy, to take up again their lost allegiance to Mother Church, he would rejoice that four souls had been saved.

But one had already died, his skin a bloody heap, his hideous body a mass of raw and bleeding flesh. Now this one had his last breath drawn shudderingly from him. Better by far, considered Father Jacinto, that if they were to die they should die

35

seemly, in a solemn auto-da-fé, so that all might witness their end and the pleas made for their recantations.

By the time Don Pedro had finished this stimulating and entertaining interlude, all four were dead. They had not died easily. Don Pedro's fat cheeks quivered in a regretful sigh as the last ladrón shrieked, blood pouring in a stream from his mouth. They could roast if they wanted. He wished merely to get his hands on more *corsarios luteranos* so that he might once again enjoy the delightful spectacle of seeing men's bodies tortured and burned and flayed and drawn.

How it stimulated a man!

With a curt word of farewell to Father Jacinto, and a gold ducat to Lorenzo, whose naked torso gleamed sweat over his fat-swathed muscles, Don Pedro hurried from the torture dungeons. He panted and puffed his way up the nitre-gleaming stairway, passing without noticing the stiff figures of the guards, and by his secret ways he passed into his suite of chambers.

Alvarez, his personal secretary, a mouse of a man dressed all in black relieved only by a thin white collar, bowed obsequiously.

"Fetch Perlita, at once! I am sharp set."

"Yes, master, at once."

Alvarez withdrew, rubbing his thin hands together, the ink stain over his right ear contrasting strangely with the white hairs at his temples. Presently he returned with Perlita, a mulatto girl of exotic body and heavy features, who knew exactly what to do to please Don Pedro. As the girl went to work on him, the happy memories of four protestants shrieking in agony filled Don Pedro with masculine vigor so that he was able to surprise even

Perlita, whose cunning hands and lascivious body provided the release for the passionate tensions the torture had built up within Don Pedro.

With a grunt Don Pedro rolled away and the girl shrank back, covering herself with the sheets. She was well schooled in white men's ways and knew they had no desire to see a woman's naked legs, even in lovemaking. Perlita wore long and wide skirts of brilliant satin, and she would lift these high for Don Pedro; she would not dream of removing them.

How her white father and her black mother had fared she did not know, although she had often wondered. Her father, a soldier who had lost an arm by some accident or other, had not confided in her, and her mother whom she remembered only as a black and sweetly scented hovering presence, had died when Perlita had been four. Now she made her way as best she could; and being in bed with the governor of San Isidro seemed to her, in her womanly wisdom, as secure a place as any on the island.

And she could curtsy so grandly to Don Pedro's fat wife as they passed in the corridors of the governmental villa—that glorious white stucco monstrosity above the waterfront! Doña Ana, fatter, shorter, stouter, more irritable, and more sweaty than her husband, had a conveniently short sight and short memory when it suited her. And, of course, there was Anton, that beautiful black buck whose position was supposed to be groom, and whose position with Doña Ana was the same as that of Don Pedro's vis-à-vis Perlita. Things passed. Life. went on. And the sun shone.

For Don Pedro, feeling his body flaccid and the sweat cold upon him, the sight of the luscious mulatto girl now convinced him how wise he had been to consent to come out to New Spain, to the island of San Isidro in the Caribbean, as the governor. He could make a fortune. He could retire to Cuba, or Hispaniola—perhaps—or go back to Castile. And, if luck smiled on him, some terrible tropical disease would carry off that fat cow of a wife of his and leave him a truly free man.

He grunted again, and sat up and snapped his fingers. Obediently Perlita slid out of the tumbled bed and brought him a glass of wine—a light dry white wine from Spain, perfectly suited to this damnable climate. He would serve his time as governor of San Isidro, and he would hang, flay, burn, rack, disembowel all the Protestant pirates his stupid sailors could catch. He would tumble Perlita, and a dozen gorgeous girls like her, and he would feel a modicum of contentment. There was always his cousin, that cold bitch Marfisa. Since her husband had died—a husband to whom she had been betrothed when both were barely out of the cradle—she had been like a lioness without cubs to guard. She should be married off and forgotten, or sent to a seminary, or lost at sea.

The money might then find its way to more deserving hands.

So Don Pedro sipped his wine, and looked at the lithe and voluptuous body of his mistress—perfectly decently clad, of course—and dreamed on his conjectures for the future.

And the strangest thing of all was that no thought of Captain Sebastian Shark crossed his scheming mind at all.

# CHAPTER FOUR

It was Harelip Quinn who first sighted the boat. He let rip a bellow that brought Captain Shark up onto the deck of *Draco*.

The sun shone down. That everlasting, terrible sun blazed and burned down upon the sea and upon the sloop and puggled men's brains in their skulls.

"Ahoy, Cap'n!" yelled Harelip Quinn. "Looks like a boatload o' corpses, mortuified, Gord 'elp 'em."

Shark sauntered slowly forward and leaped with agility into the starboard shrouds. He went up a half-dozen ratlines and hooked a cambric-sleeved arm comfortably, and then, pushing his raffish slouch hat up onto his forehead, he squinted across the dazzling sea.

Sure enough, it was a boat.

*Draco* was brought neatly alongside and buccaneers quickly hooked on lines. Shark stared down. His bronzed face under that blazing Atlantic sun—for since the Windward Passage they had left the Caribbean—grew grimmer and leaner as he surveyed the pitiful occupants of the boat.

Sun and wind had scoured the wood, so that it

lay stripped and bare, thickly encrusted with yellow-white salt deposits. Where the sea lapped the strakes the wood darkened betrayingly. The men were carefully brought out and laid upon the deck. They were nearly gone. Two were already dead and Shark checked the quick and instinctive habit of having them tossed into the sea.

"We're not in battle," he said, his voice harsh and penetrating. "At least, not at this very moment, by God! Have 'em laid out and we'll bury 'em decently."

"Aye aye, Cap'n," said Simon de Rycke. They stood looking at the six survivors.

Shark knew all about being cast adrift in an open boat with a small breaker of water and a handful of weevilly biscuits. He felt no sorrow for these men. Pity, perhaps. A feeling they had not done well in the battle of life. But they were men, as he was, and they took the same chances as he did.

One of them, his cracked lips moistened with a splash of water, managed to croak a few words.

"Thankee, Cap'n, thankee. We wuz goners, then, mark ye. Goners. The sun. . ." He rambled incoherently, and Shark gave orders to have the survivors taken below and cared for.

Flotsam of the sea, they were. Who knew how many men—aye, and women, also—had been cast adrift upon the murderous bosom of the sea?

Long Ned let rip a laugh.

"Shoulda seen their faces when we hooked on! Gord! They took us for demons from the Pit!"

The others guffawed at this. It tickled their fancy.

Shark went below to his small cabin, for *Draco* was not well endowed with accommodation. The captured ladies and their maids occupied far too much room forward of the aft cabin, turning out Simon and Pierre, although Sam Percy was no longer aboard to take up his share of the quarters. Shark slumped down on the seat running beneath the aft windows, built broad and square, and their open horn casements revealed the tumbling froth of his vessel's wake.

He had come a long way since those damned Barbary corsairs had, with the connivance of his family's enemies, snatched him away from England. Looking back, he supposed some good had come from that harsh apprenticeship, in the slave bagnios, in the galleys, learning the ways of men, learning to speak Spanish and to handle a rapier under the patient tutelage of Don Jaime, the only Spaniard for whom Sebastian cared a fig. And then Don Jaime had been betrayed by his own countrymen, too....They had been terrible days, and yet golden days, too, as Don Jaime had instructed him in all the subtle arts of the sword, using a couple of vine branches, or a couple of laths, anything that would give the feel of a rapier to his young muscles.

Now he had his own vessel, and for the nonce *Draco* suited him well enough. She was nowhere near as large or fine as *Avenger* had been, and yet she was fit for her trade. There was much in his life remaining to be done. There was Bloody Fist Hagger to be accounted for. There was Captain Wren to be thought of with fire and affection and passion—that same Captain Elizabeth Wren with whom he had fought so fiercely—in bed and out upon the Main—and who now sailed her own ship in the sweet trade as Shark sailed his.

There was much to be done if he was to amass the fortune he deemed necessary both for himself and for his crew, before he might turn his back on

41

buccaneering and return as a gentleman to England.

Mind you, a return to the Spanish Main—perhaps some sleepy Spanish town that had not heard a bell rung in warning for twenty years, with Beth Wren at his side—ah! That was a thought to make the heart beat faster!

Most buccaneers spent what little they made faster than they made it. Fortunes were not sailing about in the Caribbean waiting to be snatched up. A few hundred pounds was a sum enormously large for your average pirate, and yet a few hundred pounds would scarcely keep milady in gloves and lace in Restoration London. It was a pickle. Captain Sebastian Shark sighed, and picked up the leather-bound book from the desk by his side. Soon this damnable weather would rot the leather and dessicate the paper; but for now he could indulge his passion for John Milton.

*Draco* sailed on across a pirate sea with the brilliant and intolerant sunshine flooding into her small great cabin, and Sebastian Shark read his *Paradise Lost*. Published only in 1667 it was rare luck that a copy had come so quickly into his hands from the first edition of a mere one thousand three hundred copies. And Milton had parted with the copyright for this first imprimatur for five pounds! How could a rogue of a buccaneer hope for a fortune when a genius was paid such a paltry sum, with the promise of two additional five pounds for two further editions of the same size? But then, the blind old man with all his genius could not take a cutlass in one hand, a pistol in the other, and leap upon the deck of a fat Spanish galleon, or storm the walls of a rich Spanish-American town!

Shark turned the pages, completely absorbed, his mind far removed from the burning sea and burning sky.

Presently Patrick Murphy came in to report the survivors were well enough to speak with some sense, and they wanted to talk to the captain.

Shark sighed again, and laid the book down carefully—for from books came knowledge and with knowledge came ways and means of thwarting the damned dons—and followed the doctor out into the sunshine on deck.

Instinctively, with that seaman's blood he had inherited, he looked about the horizon, up at the set of the lugsail, felt the heel and swing of the sloop beneath him, sniffed the breeze, and was instantly in command of everything to do with his vessel.

"Ease her off a shade, Ben," he said in his quiet, perfectly modulated voice. "We don't want to run afoul of a shoal up to the nor'ard."

"Aye aye, Cap'n," said Barbados Ben, and he eased the tiller a fraction to starboard.

Then Shark turned his attention to the men he had saved from the sea.

They looked more human now, wearing rough sailor clothes given them by the buccaneers of *Draco*, and although their seamed faces were forests of whiskers still, their eyes were clear and their cracked lips glistened with water recently drunk. Water—or rum.

"Thankee, Cap'n," said the one who had previously spoken. He was a big, hunky-shouldered man and his left earlobe was tattered where a golden ring had been ripped away. "I be Lazarus Wormleigh, Cap'n, and this here be Cap'n Phillpotts, Cap'n Will Phillpotts o' *Venture Lass*, as fine a bark as you could find, aye, an' a poxy evil ship she'll be now with that devil Goliath Niven a-strutting her decks and a-callin' hisself cap'n!"

At once Shark guessed what had transpired.

43

"You are welcome aboard, Lazarus Wormleigh," he said in that cool, modulated tone. "And Cap'n Phillpotts, and the rest of you. Our duty is plain. You know what manner of vessel we are, and if I mistake me not, you are of the same calling."

"Aye, Cap'n, that we be!" said Wormleigh, with a leer.

Shark kept his temper down. He had made a mistake. He had thoughtlessly given these scarecrows the impression *Draco* was a pirate ship and he and his men were pirates. Now, if he sought to correct that impression, what would these real pirates make of it—a grown man claiming to be a lily-white buccaneer, and not an out-and-out pirate?

The captain fumed inwardly; but his lean, bronzed face betrayed nothing of that boil within him.

His muted curiosity about the silence of the man introduced as Captain Will Phillpotts was explained when Phillpotts opened his mouth. He gargled attempting to speak, gesticulating with his hands opening and closing. The man had no tongue.

"Aye, Cap'n," said Wormleigh with an eager viciousness in his tone. "That's right! That black bastard Goliath Niven tore out pore Cap'n Phillpotts' tongue, so he did, may he rot in hell and his guts turn green!"

Shark spoke a few quick conventional words of sympathy. He had not previously heard of Captain Phillpotts, or of his vessel, the bark *Venture Lass*; but that meant little. There were many freebooters and pirates operating in the Caribbean and up around the Bahamas, far too many for any but the most prominent to be generally known.

Wormleigh, when he understood who it was to whom he spoke, had heard of Captain Sebastian Shark.

"Cap'n Shark!" he said, and a delighted beaming smile spread upon his evil whiskery face. "My Gord! We'm struck lucky, we'm have, an' no mistake!"

The thing that most offended the Captain was that this Wormleigh and his comrades took Shark for a pirate, without frills, as one of themselves. This did not please Sebastian Shark. He had a reputation, yes. But he was jealous of his good name, and had no wish to be associated with your true pirate.

Their story was quickly told, although Wormleigh made of it a fine frilled and furbelowed and obscene tale. Captain Phillpotts had not been willing to make a descent on Santa Caterina, a small island where they would have to fight harder than they cared to do for a paltry reward. But the story of a great silver treasure brought into the island, a small part of the annual flota, probably, sailing up the silver sea lanes from Porto Bello as once they had sailed the gold sea lanes from Nombre de Dios, had so whetted the pirates' appetites that they had there deposed Captain Phillpotts. That had been their privilege. Under the Articles. All legal in piratical law. This giant of a man, Goliath Niven, had been at the heart of the demand, of course. And when all the speeches had been said and all the brandished cutlasses lowered, the election brought forth Goliath Niven as the new captain.

"But he had no need to cut the cap'n's tongue out, for miscalling him, the black whoreson," said Wormleigh, in full fury at the remembered outrage. "The cap'n and me, and these four stout lads, we wuz cast adrift. In that stinking open boat. Set adrift to thirst and go crazy under the sun!"

"Aye," said one of the four, a scoundrel with a cast in his left eye. He hawked and spat. "I'd like

45

to cut his tripes out, Gord knows."

"And if you spit on my deck," said Captain Shark, with that icy coldness of manner that made a man quake in his boots, "it'll be your tripes that are cut out."

The man glared at Shark as though he had not heard aright.

"What?" he said. His twisted eye gleamed in disbelief. "What, you running a king's ship, then, Cap'n?" And he guffawed hugely.

Shark was not amused.

"If we run into a Spanisher, we'll fight, an' you'll fight, lief as not. But until we do you keep the Articles of this vessel. And one is—no spitting on the decks." Shark's evil eyes fixed themselves like sucker fish on that pair of eyes gazing at him, one staring at him, the other over the larboard rail. "Aye, sonny. You remember that. Now—I'll give you a pardon, for you may not know the Articles we sail under." His eyes bored into the man. "What's your name?"

"Harley—I be William Harley—"

The man might have gone on; Shark cut him off savagely.

"William Harley—what?"

"William Harley, Cap'n." It was said sullenly.

As quickly as he had brought that murderous fury to the boil, so now the captain quelled it. He turned to his boatswain. With all that icy disdain of which he was the master, he said:

"Long Ned. D'you fetch a piece of chalk and mark a ring around that gob o' spit. When William Harley's fully recovered, put a mop into his hands. He is to clean it up." Shark swung his evil eyes about the deck. "No man else touches that filth

46

until Harley cleans it. Is that understood?"

"Aye, Cap'n," his men sang out.

The were all wearing huge beams of delight. They knew their Cap'n Shark, did they! These poor fools who'd been castaway didn't know they'd been breeched yet!

Wormleigh tried a little of bluster.

"Now, see here, Cap'n Shark—" he began.

Shark looked at him.

"We run under the Articles, Wormleigh. You wish to question them, you do with a pistol or a cutlass in your fist."

The meaning of the words was perfectly plain.

Wormleigh, who had heard of Captain Shark, had no wish at all, not the slightest desire in the whole wide world, to meet this maniacal buccaneer captain face to face in a duel of any kind.

He backed down.

He mumbled something, and as Shark opened his lips to blister the man again, Wormleigh got out a mumble sounding something like: "Meant no offense, Cap'n."

"Make it so," said Shark.

He glared around at the deck, at the set of the sail, at the sky and the clouds, sniffed the wind, bellowed a few intemperate orders that had the hands scurrying to make tidy a loose raffle of rope, and then he stalked back off his deck and so down to his cabin.

He did not feel pleased.

What a petty business it all was! Browbeating a miserable parcel of shipwrecked sailors, still weak from their ordeal. Why, that was no business for a brave, bold buccaneer. But Captain Shark had certain principles to uphold, certain remorseless sea ways that had made his name a byword among the fraternity of the coast, and no shipwrecked wretch was going to make him deviate from them. No, by God! If his men saw that bastard Harley allowed to spit on the deck, they'd all be hawking and gobbing everywhere. The reasons for Captain Shark's rules, all written fair into the Articles, were simple, and men respected him for that. He was a buccaneer. All right, if you preferred, he was a damned pirate—but he knew discipline counted in battle, and he meant to make his crew ready to answer instantly to the sound of his voice and the blow of his fist.

He picked up the Milton again; but the taste had gone, and he tossed it back onto the desk among the navigation instruments. He sighed. Paper lay there, and a fine silver inkhorn, and quills, with a fine fancy silver knife to cut them; the trouble was, he had no one to write to. The loneliness of his life struck in shrewdly on him then, and he forced himself to sit up—for standing without hunching over was impossible in that low overhead—and he bellowed for Tom Bowling.

"Aye, Cap'n—what is it you'll be wantin' now?"

"Fetch a posset o' rum, Tom, there's a good fellow. I'm out o' sorts and I'd like to—to—"

Tom Bowling chuckled.

"To spit ta knave or a fair wench, Cap'n. Aye, I know. Tom Bowling knows, does Tom Bowling."

"Fetch it, you rascal!" bellowed Shark, and he snatched a sea boot and hurled it at Tom's head. Tom guffawed and slid out of the door, and the sea boot thudded into the panel. Shark let out a great whoosh of air, and laughed.

By God! A little fracas with faithful Tom, and he felt better already.

But, all the same, Tom was right.

To plunge into the battle smoke, to cross swords with a redoubtable foeman! Or, more sweetly, to seize up Captain Beth Wren in his arms! Aye!

That made him fall to brooding on the dark-eyed señorita aboard, that she-cat Isabella Urraca Castileja de la Cuerva, and only the timely entrance of Tom with the rum prevented him from bawling out on deck and creating havoc with his good intentions.

The quicker the Spanish women were off his vessel the better. And, for the discomfort they were causing him, he'd double their ransoms!

# CHAPTER FIVE

The noise racketing out from The Red Dog could have been heard from one end of the waterfront to the other. It could have. But it was not. Two doors away from The Red Dog the noise blasting from The Golden Swan not only drowned the Red Dog's offering but added its own quota. And three doors in the other direction The Licentious Lady poured a solid bellow of sound out over the waterfront and, joining with all the other taverns and ale houses and inns and just plain whorehouses, filled the night sky with pandemonium. The glowing stars seemed to flicker in the rocking din.

When buccaneers and pirates caroused, they wanted everyone in this safe anchorage to know it.

"Rum!" was the cry. "Brandy!" Other exotic drinks were recklessly tossed down, and no one cared if they mixed or did not mix. If a drunk became too hard to handle there was always a willing gang of pirates to hurl him into the gutter, for the price of a fresh jug and the sheer fun of it. Money changed hands in an endless stream. Here during the day sober merchants might strike deals with the pirates for their ill-gotten hauls; the evening and the night were the times for the pirates to spend their gold and silver as quickly as they could.

No one bothered to save, for tomorrow they might be sinking all agurgle with the shattered timbers of their ships, or dangling in irons in Execution Dock, or screaming their guts out in a Spanish Inquisition prison. So! Drink, cullies, drink and be merry, for tomorrow. . .

In the lantern lights of the taverns, the alleys and byways lay shrouded in a deeper darkness, peopled by creatures of the night—pickpockets, thieves, whores, broken men, slaves, pimps. And if those tavern lights picked out the golden glint of an earring or the flash of a great jewel on a coarse finger, why, it needed a tough pair of arms, a heavy boot and a quick pistol, a handy rapier or cutlass, to defend a man's body and possessions.

Captain Shark strode up to The Red Dog and roared with laughter when he saw the lean shapes lurking in the shadows. His face was flushed, his mustaches abristle.

"Here, you dogs!" he bellowed. He tossed a handful of silver broadcast and roared his merriment again. "You'll know Cap'n Shark's ashore!"

"Aye, aye, Cap'n!" The creatures of the night shuffled forward eagerly, snuffling, crouching to dart at the coins. Not one wanted to be the first. The first was likely to get a knife in his back for his pains.

Shark let roar his great booming laugh again.

"Faith!" said Captain Shark. "The rascals have sense enough not to trust one another."

"Let 'em all go hang," said Pierre Depoix, fluttering his scent-soaked lace kerchief to his nostrils.

"Aye, Cap'n," said Simon de Rycke. "Why encourage their whining?"

51

"As to that, my friends, I give you this thought. If they have silver they will drink themselves stupid on some foul house this night. And so when we stagger back to *Draco*, as drunk as lords. I'll wager they will not be around to stick a knife in our backs."

His two lieutenants gaped at him. Shark knew that was all nonsense, of course; there were many more than the few to whom he had flung the silver; but the conceit was one of those conundrums of human behavior with which he liked to idle away his time between forays.

"Well, Cap'n," cut in Long Ned, who kept licking his lips. "Which 'un is it to be, then?"

Shark's great laugh boomed out again. He halted and stood before Long Ned, who looked up into the night sky, and down at the mud and slosh, and around at the lighted windows and the uproar bellowing along the waterfront.

"Again, Ned? If you really fancy Fat Freda at The Charles's Head—why, then, go to her, man!"

"It ain't that, Cap'n—"

"We're for The Red Dog, Ned," sang out Pierre.

Long Ned hesitated. He wanted to sing and carouse with his companions, but he also wanted to get his arms around Fat Freda, and start to work on her. He hesitated, shifting from one foot to the other.

"Come on, Cap'n!" yelled Simon, his Flemish voice strong in the night.

"*Corbleu*! I am with you, Simon!" And Pierre hitched his rapier up and stamped his elegant boots after Simon.

"You see how it is, Ned—"

"Oh, aye! I see!" Long Ned picked his nose, nibbled, swore with pleasant fluidity and coarseness, and started after his comrades. "Fat Freda c'n wait! I need a drink."

If no one mentioned that drinks were quite easily obtainable in The Charles's Head tavern—as easily, really, as at The Red Dog—they forebore out of delicate questions of sentimentality. The notion that one hardened pirate would sooner drink with his comrades than chase after skirt would have struck them as droll.

So Long Ned, with a copious delivery of spittle into the gutter, followed on.

The wall of sound, heat, smoke, and light hit them as they barged in through the door. At once they were greeted by a raucous yelling from all over the tavern. Fierce yells of greeting and violent declarations of friendship slit the thick air. Glasses and pewter pots appeared miraculously in a swirl of white petticoats. A table and benches were found, and a great chair for the captain. Shark buried his nose in the rum pot and swallowed, and roared his great laugh.

"By thunder! That sets a man up, does that!"

Captain One Eye Turling blustered forward, one hand twisting his beard, the other outstretched. Shark shook hands and felt the sinewy strength.

"It's good to see you, Cap'n Shark. I've had but one miserable Spanisher these last four weeks, and I'm fair famished. Tell us you bring good news."

"Aye," yelped a thin, stooped man with a livid sear down one cheek that ripped the corner of his mouth into a permanent leer. "We'm a hungry for Spanishers."

"I saw but one, Lemuel," said the captain, and his mild tone took them aback.

"One, Cap'n Shark!"

"Aye. We took her, in fine style, and then the

mangy cur scuttled herself. Sank herself right under us. We were in a fair way to getting our breeches wet."

They guffawed at this, and the tale was told. But Shark did not mention the five ladies, and no one else from *Draco* would do so, for fear of the consequences.

Shark's familiar broad black hat with the silver gray feather lay on the table before him, and any man foolish enough to spill ale or rum upon it would find six inches of Toledo steel sticking from his front through his back. Everyone knew this. That hat could go through hellfire and brimstone and not come to harm. Normally Shark wore a deep blue coat, and breeches of the same color stuffed down into his black boots. However, for this night Shark had donned a brave scarlet coat rich with gold facings and loaded with a massive frill of finest lace foaming at his throat and sleeves. He looked that archetype of danger, the villainous gentleman, or the gentlemanly villain.

But he was no gentleman in his own estimation, and he could not conceive of himself as anything less than thoroughly villainous. Who but a villain would have treated Señorita Isabella as he had?

Now he leaned negligently upon his elbow in that inferno of noise and smoke, with the rum fumes and the brandy fumes coiling, and watched as the wenches ran with their pewter trays loaded with more drinks, and chuckled as a sly hand slipped up a skirt to pinch a rounded bottom. Very convivial, was Captain Shark this night. Very open to a jest or a story, ready to laugh at anything and at nothing.

If he gave a thought to his copy of Milton, lying closed on his cabin desk, it did not show upon his lean and rakish face. He twirled his mustaches from time to time, and quaffed his rum, and greeted acquaintance after acquaintance as they came over to exchange news and bawdy jests, and propose schemes of joint conquest that would infallibly make them all richer than those old gold-plated Incas.

"Faith, Houndsditch Harry! If I went with ye up agin Porto Bello, what would the señoritas o' Nombre de Dios say, eh? Mark me that, you ruffian!"

And Houndsditch Harry opened wide his bearded lips and bared a vast cavity fringed with the rotting reminders of ancient fangs, and he roared out a foul effluvium borne on his belly laughter.

"You allus was a wag, Cap'n Shark!"

"Aye, but mark me you this, Harry." And Shark leaned closer across the table, and those around them stilled their laughter at his cold and savage words. "We're coming to an end o' the Caribbean, Harry. It's the Pacific side o' the Main for us—it's been done before. And, by God, to smash the Spanishers we'll take the Gold Road again—aye, and what's upon the Gold Road, sink me else!"

"Aye!" they roared, stamping their feet, banging upon the tables, making the pewter pots dance and spill foaming suds. "Aye! It's the Pacific for us, and to hell with the dons!"

One man sat pushed back in his chair, with an ebony cane, flaunting a gay red ribbon beneath its gold top, supporting his easy and angular frame against the table. He wore dark clothes with silver lace, and his huge black peruke framed and shadowed a thin, intense face in which the eyes gleamed like live coals. There was much about this man that aped the demeanor of Captain Shark himself. The rapier swinging at his side from an elaborately embroidered baldric proclaimed him a fighter; but the difference here between his appearance and that of Shark was that Shark's baldric was a plain black leather affair, much worn and scuffed from long wear.

"Oho," said this man, letting his cane slip and bringing the front legs of his chair to the floor with a crash. "So the brave Captain Shark wishes to lead more men to their deaths crossing the Isthmus!"

A silence fell—a deathly silence, for, at once and unmistakably, everyone present knew the end of this must be death.

Casually, Captain Shark turned his left wrist to let the foam of lace fall. He idly turned his hand toward the thin man in the chair, who now sat thrust forward, his burning eyes fixed upon Shark.

"And who, pray, is this fellow?" inquired Shark of the tavern at large.

A sibilant whisper of indrawn breaths came as a reply that did not enlighten him on the man's name; but well enough enlightened him on the man's reputation.

At last, in a creaking silence, the man parted his thin lips. He had a smooth voice; but Shark detected the hectoring tone beneath the words, the habitual way of talking that took no reck of human dignity.

"I know you, Captain Shark. You betrayed Captain Lightfoot and sold him to the dons! Oh, yes, Shark, I know you for the condemned, thieving, piratical rat you are."

A keen observer might have noticed the skin beneath Shark's eyes tighten; that was all the change he would have observed in the Captain's demeanor.

Shark turned to face the man. He spoke in a low, insolent drawl.

"I wondered who you were, sir. Now I know.

You are a foul and stinking body-louse crawled from the arsehole of the Devil himself."

At this, Long Ned let rip a cackle that was instantly quelled as Simon gave him a kick upon the ankle.

"This is a killing matter, imbecile!" whispered Pierre.

The man in black pushed his chair back with a loud and dramatic scraping of wood upon wood. He stood and threw back the heavy skirts of his coat. With a single long screech of metal his rapier glittered in his hand.

"Whoreson dog!", he yelled. He had quite forgotten his cool manners. "I'll split your belly through to your backbone and spit upon your corpse!"

"As to that," said Sebastian, rising gently, his right hand moving across his body and settling onto the old familiar hilt of his rapier, "why, sir, you are at perfect liberty to try."

Then, as an afterthought, and before he drew, he added: "In which order, sir, would you wish to understand your use of the form 'spit'?"

"*Parbleu!*" whispered Pierre. "Draw, mon capitaine!"

Still Shark stood there, kicking his great chair back with one booted foot, his hand across his body. He did not smile and all the laugh lines had fled from his face.

"You will scream and grovel, you black bastard, Shark! And I'll stamp on your face—"

The man threw himself on guard and then, instantly and without a salute, went into the lunge position and drove with full murderous intent upon the captain.

Sebastian's hand moved with a speed that left the onlookers blinking.

One instant this unknown but reputable adversary

was driving his point toward Shark's midriff; the next moment a silver twinkling bar of steel appeared as though by magic to twitch that seeking rapier away. With a slender flourish and a circle, Shark's blade licked at his opponent's wrist and drew blood, which seeped into the fine, white lace.

"You'll scream, Shark, you'll beg for mercy—"

"A pox on you, too, you tiresome dog!"

And Shark sent his rapier into a blinding series of passades and beats and feints which halted the other's attack. But Shark did not press, and twice, when he could see he had an opening, he did not lunge and finish it. He was intrigued. So the rapiers clinked and scraped with sudden fierce bursts of wrist-power, and the booted feet stamped, now forward, now back, all in line and firmly yet lightly balanced. Shark wanted to know this lunatic's story before he killed him.

And, of course, there was always the possibility that it would be Shark himself who was killed. Always, that possibility yawned before the captain when he became embroiled in a fight of this nature. But, then, that was the spice of life. That gave the fight a zest. If he knew every time he fought he was going to win—where would be the fun of that?

Also, at the rear of the hastily formed ring of pirates and wenches, all gaping at the duel, there stood a number of men Shark did not know. That meant nothing, for he could not expect to know every cutthroat in the West Indies. But he knew instinctively these were men of this maniac's crew. They would pistol him if he won too easily. He had to get word to Pierre and Simon and Long Ned to take care of them.

So, as he fought, Captain Shark maneuvered his

man around that ring of shouting onlookers, feinting here, slipping there, circling, circling, and so came close to Pierre.

"Those four apes by Buxom Bessie, Pierre. Settle 'em!"

"Oui, mon capitaine! With the pleasure!"

As his own men eased back to take care of the four Shark could let himself take a greater interest in the fight.

This character was a great swordsman. He possessed a wrist of steel, and three times Shark almost let him through. The man sensed his own power. He laughed, quickly, eagerly, and pressed with great vigor, letting his strength do the work required of skill. Shark gave ground. He backtracked. He kept the other off with a cunning display of superb skill he masked under a few apparently clumsy and desperate counters.

Now he saw four men at the back of the ring go suddenly stiff, lifting hands which clawed for help to an unresponsive heaven, and allowing their pistols to clatter to the floor. The sound was lost in the hullabaloo racketing up from the engrossed onlookers.

Shark chuckled. He had told his men to settle the four. They had done the job with knives in the back or sides, just under the ribs. Well, that was the pirate way. . .

Now Shark let a quick thrust from his adversary go perilously close to his left side. He circled his own blade, contacted, slid with a scrape of steel and then, with a quick beat, circled the other way. Now his own wrist of steel hardened. He flurried a few quick passes and caught another thrust, and then disdainfully bent as the fool slashed his rapier across in a wide stroke aimed at taking his head off, most likely. That kind of slashing style was going out of style; it had long since been abandoned by masters of the art.

Now the man's eyes widened.

He took a step back.

His blade faltered, and then came up to counter as Shark threatened to drive home. But Shark's blade was not where his adversary expected it. Instead, that long and lethal blade struck through low, clear of bone, and drove on through the man's belly. It jerked out through the back, spouting blood and bits of gristle. Shark stepped back, withdrawing his blade.

The man in the black and silver costume stood upright, a look of the utmost amazement upon his face.

Then he dropped his rapier. He bent in the middle. Before he could get his hands to his guts he toppled on his face and rolled over on to his side. He was not dead. But he would be, soon enough.

Shark bent to him. The shouting died.

"Captain Lightfoot, you said?"

"Aye." the words came out with a gasp, but without blood. Shark's rapier had struck too low for blood from the lungs. "Aye—a comrade—and you sold him—"

"No," said Shark in his quiet conversational tone. "No, my friend. He sold himself. He attempted to betray me and was taken in his own snare."

"You lie."

"I have already killed you once. It would be tiresome to have to kill you again, my friend. I do not lie."

"I—I—I was told—"

"You were told lies. But, before you die, tell me.

Who are you?"

"I am Captain Gore. Captain Rafe Gore. An' I'll remember you in hell, Cap'n Shark!"

"Oh, aye. Remember. And while you're at it get a place ready for me there, too. Find a nice quiet spot where it's not too hot. We can talk over old times."

But Captain Gore's eyes closed and he lay back, breathing in dreadful gasping whoops. Shark straightened up.

"The fool should not have believed all he was told." He bent again and carefully wiped his blade upon the fine white and silver lace. He was thorough. During all this no one spoke. He straightened up again. "Give him a decent burial. I will pay the charges. Now, landlord! Fill the glasses. Charge your ugly faces, all! A bumper! Let us drink a toast. To hell and damnation to the Spanish!"

"Aye!" The answering roar near lifted the roof. "Aye, Cap'n Shark! *Cap'n Shark!*"

# CHAPTER SIX

The flat smack of a signal gun from the ramparts brought Don Pedro up with a start. His naked legs, fat and sweaty, lay entangled with the golden brown legs of Perlita, and his body was enmeshed with hers. He grunted and levered himself up, cursing.

"Now if that is some stupid fool of a soldier who has fired off the culverin by mistake I will hang and jerk him! I swear by the Virgin of Campanella!"

"You are going, Don Pedro," said Perlita, in a small voice. Don Pedro never liked to be reminded of the rapidity with which he shrank.

"Devil take it!" Don Pedro flailed around searching for his breeches. He was unwilling for Valence, his valet, to find him in so undignified a posture at this time in the afternoon. At night, of course, it was a matter of honor for Valence to be summoned afterwards, so that Don Pedro could smirk and stroke his mustaches, the proud accomplisher of great feats. But he'd been suddenly smitten this afternoon as Perlita had bent over to gather her little puppy into her arms, an affectation she had copied from the great ladies, who in their turn had copied it from home. The sight of the rounded and smooth expanse of her bosom had suddenly—and with joyful unexpectedness driven a white-hot rapier of pain into his loins. So he had begun—and some fool had let off the warning gun.

He struggled into his breeches. Perlita, all breathless and contrite, helped him pull on his boots.

"Your rapier, my lord!" And: "Your peruke, my lord!" And: "Your snuff box, your kerchief, your cane, my lord!"

By the time his fat body was accoutred to face the inquisitive stares of the common soldiery and their damned affected officers, enough time had passed for the galleons to have made good headway into the bay past the stone fort.

Don Pedro stepped out onto his broad paved patio and snapped irritably at the servants who came running, then he swung nastily upon Captain da Silva, the officer of the day.

"Three ships, my lord. They are Spanish—"

A great weight lifted from Don Pedro's heart.

He said: "Of course! You idiot—had they been English I would have given orders to send them to bottom at once!"

He strutted away down to the waterfront and, standing in the shade of the waiting shelter there, stared across the water. Captain Alvarez had already taken a boat out to meet the incoming ships. Anchors roared their cables through hawseholes, the water churned as the bumboats circled, waiting for permission to come alongside. Presently the boat returned with Captain Alvarez in the sternsheets, looking especially stiff and correct. At his side sat a tall, elegant hidalgo, smothered in lace, wearing a yellow suit of taffeta, a monstrous peruke, and a broad-brimmed hat sporting a scarlet feather.

When this man leaped lithely onto the stones and gave the governor an elegant bow, Don Pedro judged the depth of that bow and knew he faced a man who considered himself important.

The introductions were made.

Then Don Pedro knew, indeed, that the good God had sent either an angel or a devil to assist him in his never-ending fight against the *corsarios*.

This was Don Hernandez, Marquis of Requanza.

"I bear full authority, Don Pedro, to require you to assist me in every way possible in the suppression of these infernal *corsarios luteranos*."

"You are most welcome, Marquis, most welcome. Believe me, as governor of San Isidro, I shall do all in my power to assist you."

Neither man missed the significance of that interpolation; Don Pedro was the governor, and this newcomer, with all his steel and velvet and his orders, must recognize that.

Don Hernandez flicked his elegantly laced cuff in the sunshine as they went up to the governor's palatial villa. He was well aware of the figure he cut. Still not yet thirty, he had kept himself in the full vigor of his manhood, tough, competent, aggressive, arrogant. He possessed a wrist of steel, a will of steel, and a heart of steel. He fully intended to cut the *demonios* into little pieces and hang each several piece from the yardarms of his ships. He knew what he was going to do. He was a man, was Don Hernandez, who kept his word and did what he promised.

So far.

Don Pedro had immediately formed one distinct impression of this formidable marquis, and the moment they were within doors and out of that wretched sunshine he gave whispered and urgent

64

instructions to Valence to keep Perlita away and out of sight. Don Pedro's fat wife was introduced, all rolling flesh and sweat, and Alvarez, his personal secretary, was indicated with a negligent wave of a fat, white hand.

Father Jacinto required greater courtesy in the introductions, and Don Pedro watched keenly as the marquis and the priest sized each other up. There was steel and flint here, and from these could be struck fire. Don Pedro, fat, and sweating, and ineffectual, watched and hoped. . .

The marquis had brought a small suite with him, and of this staff of gallant officers only one man impressed Don Pedro. This was a pale-faced man, whose face saw more of the lantern-lit cabins than the decks. He had that piercing darkness to his eyes, and that shadow around them, that informed Don Pedro that this was a fanatic of a stripe far worse than Father Jacinto. Father Dominic—for he had taken that name at the seminary—said nothing. His ashen lips and thin nose reminded Don Pedro of some underground monster, forever scenting prey in the dark. Don Pedro found it expedient for the two Fathers to walk and talk together, a little apart from the hidalgos, the fighting men, and the ladies.

When in the due course of hospitality they sat to a meal the conversation remained strained. Those men who had spent some time in the West Indies regarded new arrivals, for all their force and their fine ships, with rancorous humor. When they'd been out in this hellhole for a space they'd understand more of the problems, by the Virgin! The *corsarios* were a menace; but so was the heat, and the disease, and the ever-pestilent fly. The talk rumbled on around the table. A messenger was announced.

"We'll surprise them in their own foul nests!"

Don Juan Valdez was proclaiming in his loud and blustering way when the messenger was announced. This Don Juan Valdez commanded one of the marquis' ships, and, of course, he had a shipmaster and crew to sail the vessel; Don Juan and his soldiers would fight, but would never put a hand to a rope or a capstan bar.

Don Pedro, looking up, saw Don Garcia de Montija hobble through the door.

Don Garcia's lined face showed a terrible and consuming anger. His dark eyes glittered upon the assembled company with bitter contempt.

"And you sit here, drinking your wine and lolling at your ease, and talk about the king's enemies upon the seas! By the Holy Mother of God! Do you not know what they do! Why do you not sail immediately and tear their foul hearts from their vile breasts?"

Don Pedro rose with fat haste. He knew Don Garcia of old. They had become better acquainted over the past few years only through the friendship of Don Pedro's cousin, the Duchess Marfisa, and Don Garcia's niece, Isabella Castileja. Don Garcia, as all who knew him would testify, was short-tempered and arrogant and intolerant of mistakes. His own belief in his pride and honor was a tangible presence about him. He would maintain his honor in the face of the very devil himself.

"Don Garcia!" said Don Pedro, his oily features writhing into a fatuous smile. "Come, come, old friend. Step in. I would like to present you to Don Hernandez, the Marquis of Requanza."

That was clear warning, surely. Now Don Garcia should stop his hectoring tone and speak more civilly, by God!

"Yes, I have heard of Don Hernandez." Don

Garcia spoke with less hatred now, but the boiling torment of pain that had brought him here persisted. "I understand you command these great ships in the harbor, Don Hernandez. I ask you, then, why they are not at sea, hunting down these *demonios*, these defilers, these ravishers, these—"

"What has happened, Don Garcia?" demanded Don Pedro.

"I will tell you what has happened. I have had word—just arrived—I have ridden here from the other side of the island to tell you personally. The convoy was scattered. The last the admiral saw of *Doña Rosaria*, a devil-spawned pirate sloop was creeping up on her—"

Don Pedro crossed himself.

A hushed silence fell upon those at the brilliant table.

"The ship was—" Don Pedro swallowed, "was taken?"

"Yes, Taken! The reports are now certain. The ship was taken. By *corsarios*! And you know, Don Pedro, who sailed in her!"

Don Pedro's fat cheeks sagged.

He slumped back in his great carved chair and with unsteady hands he poured a glass of brandy.

"Drink!" spat Don Garcia in contempt. "That will not bring my Isabella back—or your cousin, Marfisa!"

Don Hernandez, Marquis of Requanza, stood up, his right hand outstretched, his left gripping the hilt of the rapier he had not unbuckled when he sat down to eat.

"The Duchess Marfisa de Ariza?"

"Who else, Marquis, who else?" Don Garcia was past caring for the forms of etiquette so precious to the hidalgo. "She was entrusted out of our hands to the sea, and she has been taken—taken—by a *demonio*—taken and ravished!"

"I will draw that man's internal body out through his stomach. I will hang him, I will flay him, I will—" Don Hernandez caught himself. He held his passion in with a fierce willpower that forced deep white indentations into the sides of his nostrils. He had come to New Spain to command the few fresh ships spared him to sweep the seas of *corsarios*; but, also—and far sweeter—he had taken this long journey to seek the hand of the Duchess Marfisa. He had loved her since the moment he had first seen her, at her wedding to that fool of a boy, the Duke of Medelina.

Everyone was looking at him. He forced himself to adopt the haughty look of absolute power that he was accustomed to showing to the world. Later he would mourn for his lost Marfisa. Then a thought occurred to him, a thought like a draught of sweet water to a man on a deserted island.

"There has been a demand for ransom?" Before Don Garcia could answer, he rattled on: "I will pay! I will pay all that they demand. Then, afterwards, I will hang and draw and quarter—"

"Marquis!" interrupted Don Pedro, shoving his fat form up from the carved chair. "The duchess is my cousin! I should pay the ransom demand, in all honor, sir!"

"It matters not who pays," said Don Garcia, limping to the table and taking up a glass of brandy at random. He had been wounded long ago and still limped as a memento of standing in the way of English roundshot. "There has been no demand for ransom. No word has been received from the Duchess, or from Isabella, or their confidante."

It crossed the mind of Don Hernandez, the

Marquis, to ask in his most evil way just why the ladies had been allowed to take a sea journey. But he forebore. To ask that was to betray too openly the broken reed that once had been Spanish sea-power.

They sat around the table, or stood hot in their anger, these high-born hidalgos of Spain, gorgeous in satins and taffetas, in silks and velvets, the splendid Toledo blades at their hips, their perukes black and curled. They swore and blasphemed and beat the table with their clenched fists and promised to sail on the morrow, straightaway, to avenge this dastardly deed. Of them all, perhaps only one man—and he a poor hidalgo called Don Mercurio, sitting partly isolated at the end of the table—saw with a clearer eye the true picture these men presented.

As an adventurer whose illustrious forebears had squandered their heritage and bequeathed to him only a name—which he refused to employ, contenting himself with the name Don Mercurio, and a blade of finest Toledo steel, Don Mercurio had been forced to seek his fortune in the world. Where better to find fame and fortune than in New Spain? So he was a member of the soldiery assigned to protect this wealthy island of San Isidro, and the boredom and monotony of his existence near drove him mad. Only the bed of some complaisant woman—and there were many who would favor Don Mercurio—or a vicious and swiftly fought battle, could raise his drooping spirits. He drank sparingly. He ate moderately. He kept himself clean and fit. But, like them all, the climate was wearing him down.

He sat and studied these compañeros of his, did Don Mercurio, and he sighed, and considered again the treacherous thought that the English and their

Protestant allies had all the luck in this half of the world.

There was Don Garcia de Montija, hobbling about and swearing eternal damnation upon the despoilers of his niece Isabella. Don Mercurio stroked his mustaches, but he did not smile. There was fat and stupid Don Pedro, trying to prevent insults and challenges from flying in his own banquet hall. There was this newly arrived popinjay, Don Hernandez, the Marquis of Requanza, with fine ships under his command, promising to bring the *corsarios* to a swift destruction....Don Mercurio leaned elegantly at the table, eating an orange with a silver knife, and considered the other man. Don Hernandez looked capable, cold, and cruel, like a man who would drive his servants to the point of death, and beyond.

Now, if by chance some accident befell one of Hernandez's officers, and a certain bravo called Don Mercurio just happened to be there in the right place at the right time, a more interesting phase of life might begin. Don Mercurio cut with the little silver knife, and sucked the rich juice, and pondered the problem. He was ambitious; but he also valued his own hide. There had to be ways and ways, and he considered he was clever-witted enough to encompass his own ambitions within the silver glitter of the circle about the marquis.

The hubbub and the drinking went on. The promises were made in grandiloquent form. The great ships fresh from Spain would go about their master's business and sweep the seas clean as they had been clean long ago, when they were the entire property of Spain. Even Portugal no longer belonged to Spain. But the Portuguese had their own dominions and spheres of interest to worry about;

70

they need not come into the calculations.

"Wood and water, food, fresh fruit and vegetables, and we sail!" declared the marquis. He had drunk deeply, but he was in perfect control of himself—a dangerous man. "We have full shot-lockers and our powder tiers are fully loaded. We will blow the *corsarios* out of the water and then we will know how to deal with what is left."

"I shall look forward to that," said Don Pedro, his eyes glinting at the prospect of fresh fodder for his torture dungeons below the fortress.

"I wish you Godspeed for the morrow, Don Hernandez."

The fates of the Duchess Marfisa, and of Isabella, already were of the past, and best forgotten. Revenge was now what mattered, that and sweeping the seas clean. Don Garcia licked his lips.

"Honor!" he whispered. "The honor of our house must be maintained!"

"Fill my dungeons with shrieking heretics!" were the thoughts of Don Pedro.

"My ships and my soldiers will scour the Caribbean!" boasted Don Hernandez.

And Don Mercurio watched them, lazily, and totted up the best chances of a broken neck being found in a dark alleyway or in an unexpected fall down the long marble flight of stairs.

# CHAPTER SEVEN

Captain Sebastian Shark always considered sailors to be a strange breed of men.

They spent their lives apart from the major part of humanity, adrift upon an element unnatural to men, sailing the oceans at the whims of wind and tide. They developed their own ways, sea ways, and they spoke their own language, sea language.

The old shellback could smell a gale coming up long before the sky grew brassy and the wind died.

Shark stood upon his own deck as *Draco* drove on southerly across the Caribbean, his thoughts dwelling on the best means of raising the ransom demands for the Spanish ladies higher, and these thoughts jumbled with plans to careen the sloop. He carried charts of the Caribbean in his head, with the hidden creeks, where he could find wood and water and careen his ship, mentally marked in red, like the holy days in a calendar.

He sniffed.

He turned with lean and elegant poise to where John Fakenham stood by the weather bulwarks.

"Pass the word for Long Ned, if you please, John."

John Fakenham expressed no surprise at his captain's form of words. Had not the young lad Fakenham ridden with Cromwell's Ironsides? Did he not understand the niceties and the etiquettes of command and of war?

"Aye aye, Cap'n."

Soon Long Ned came aft, still chewing, the fat dribbling down his chin.

Shark had no need to say anything as his boatswain looked up at the sky and over to the weather horizon, and, then, critically, across to the western rim of the sea.

"Aye, Cap'n. You'm right. There'll be a blow."

"See to it, Ned. Batten everything down."

"Aye aye, Cap'n."

There was no need to give explicit orders. The boatswain knew what to do, and Simon or Pierre would go around to make sure everything was done properly. Shark ran what would have been called in the Royal Navy a taut ship. For all that he was dubbed a pirate, Shark knew what he knew about seafaring, and he knew that there was only one way to stay alive when the elements raged and tore at his vessel.

A note of extra attention to detail sounded aboard and soon *Draco* was snugged down, her single lugsail all ready to be so maneuvered as to give her steerage way without tearing itself to pieces. The sky turned a bilious green bronze and the wind died, but the sure seafaring instincts of the captain told him this would be no serious blow. The gale, when at last it roared in low and level across the sea, was no West Indian hurricane, no colossal upheaval of the elements. Despite that, *Draco* pitched on her nose and tail, and rolled vilely, and the experience made Shark think very closely about the advisability of acquiring a larger vessel. Three masts, he had proved, were the best. Since the scrapping of the bonaventure mizen and the general adoption of topgallants, ships had tended to become stodgy and bulky and heavy. But, with a little careful trimming and balancing, Shark knew he could make a racehorse out of any reasonable hull. He mused, as the seas rose violently, and the wind cut the spindrift from the waves, and the whole world revolved.

On the morrow, with not a speck of land in sight and the sun drawing the moisture from the sea in level swathes of brilliant light, the old faithful grades eased their way back and the lugsail rose to its full extent up the mast, and *Draco* surged heavily over a still sullen sea. The swell remained, driving the sloop down into steep alleyways of waves and lifting her high atop steeple-spires of water.

"It's a morning to be alive, Pierre!" quoth Captain Shark, expanding that incredibly broad chest of his and drawing in rib-creaking lungsful of air. "My oath on't!"

"Aye, mon capitaine! But the ladies fared ill, I am not at all sorry to say. . ."

"Hale 'em out. We'll see if the ocean has loosened their tongues."

Accustomed to sea travel aboard a large and opulent galleon, Isabella had spent a ferociously miserable night. As the tiny vessel had swooped and rolled and surged in the water she had thought every second would be her last. The maids and the confidante had shrieked and swooned. Marfisa, as befitted a duchess, had retained her icy and aloof air of total composure. But when she had belched out her stomach's contents in a green and viscous

© Lorillard 1975

If you have
a taste for quality,
you'll like the taste
of Kent.

King Size
or Deluxe 100's.

KENT

WITH
THE FAMOUS MICRONITE FILTER

KING SIZE

KING SIZE
KENT

stream, even she had given in and sobbed with heartbreaking despair.

So Shark got little from the ladies of Spain that forenoon. The bells struck the half hours, as was proper, and the vessel cleaned up and maintained the kind of discipline which had made Shark's name a byword among the Brotherhood of the Coast. His own men understood the value of Shark's ways. The day wore on and still that sea kept up, long, green, marbled rollers surging across the wind and making life as uncomfortable as it usually was. Isabella could eat little. The tiny cramped hole in which the women were confined choked her. Her body felt unclean. She was famished with hunger and thirst, and yet her stomach revolted at the idea of food.

Toward evening Shark called the women on deck again and, having heard from Surgeon Murphy of their complaints, sternly bade them eat something.

"For the love of God, ladies!" he said, his exasperation transparent. "I am not going to murder you! I merely wish to relieve the thieving dogs of Spanishers, your relatives, of some gold on your account. If you die in my ship—" A thought struck him then, whereat he smiled most evilly. "If you die in my ship through willful disobedience to God's commands—"

Isabella translated in quick and jerky stabs as Shark paused. Now she in her turn paused. She glared at him in the fading light.

"What do you know of God's commands, you heretical Englishman?"

"I know this, Doña Isabella—that God in your heathen beliefs does not care to welcome a suicide into the eternal life. If you die willfully here you will commit suicide and imperil your immortal souls!"

Isabella gasped. Marfisa pressed her to **translate.**
When she had done so, Isabella put a hand to her
eyes. Shark watched, unsmiling, his thin lips closed.
The Duchess Marfisa clenched her fists. *"Lobos
marinos!"* she said. But the venom sank into a wall
of despair.

Shark wasn't prepared to see a silly parcel of girls
commit suicide and cheat him out of rich Spanish
gold. No, by God!

He said: "The food is good. We are not some
filthy merchantman with foul water and weevilly
biscuits and stinking beef in barrel for year after
year. You call us pirates—well, we live well! We take
fresh food and fruits and we have good boucanned
meat. There is no pleasure in eating as poor honest
sailormen do. Se eat your fill, or I'll have my men
prize open your jaws and force the food down your
gullets!"

What the Captain said about the food at sea was
true. If the truth was told, many and many a poor
devil had taken up piracy because he could no
longer stomach the foul food dished out aboard
merchant ships as well as king's ships. If the
wealthy merchants and the admirals treated their
seamen properly, as they deserved, then there would
be far fewer pirates roaming the seas.

*"Lobos marinos!"* wailed Marfisa, again, her
hands covering her face, and shaking, shaking. . .

"We may be sea wolves, Doña Marfisa," said
Shark, and he admitted to himself that he spoke
churlishly. "But I want you alive and well and
ready to run to the arms of your family."

When Isabella translated that, Marfisa let a shocking shriek of agony burst from her. "My family!"
she screamed. "Poor fool! Animal! What do you
know of my family! My stupid husband is dead, a

mere boy and without weapons. I am tossed about this dreadful sea, and when I try to escape you—you *demonio*!—you take me up and, and—"

"Ha!" said Shark. He spoke even as Isabella was translating, shaken by the Duchess's outburst. Shark smoothed the quirky line from his lips; he still did not wish Isabella to know he understood pure Castilian as well as she did.

"And the only man for whom I care—Don Hernandez—where is he! In Spain, pining for me—and I—I—"

There would have been a lot more of it, but Shark ordered the women below. He would not acknowledge that he was embarrassed. What! He—a tough, rough, piratical old sea dog, embarrassed by a girl screaming her tortured life's problems out on his deck? Never!

And there was always the duchess's cousin, this Don Pedro who was governor of San Isidro. . . Someone existed who would pay a ransom for the duchess.

Harelip Quinn, perched uncomfortably at the summit of the ratlines where a top should rightfully be, hailed the deck.

"Deck there! There's a tops'l a-hoverin' on th' horison, Cap'n. Won't come nigh nor won't go down."

Well, that ship out there might be an honest merchantman, an Englishman, or a Frenchman, or a Dutchman, or even, a Dane. They were all safe from the depredations of Captain Shark. She might be a Spanisher. Ah, now, there was a thought to set the blood racing through a man's veins. Or, of course, she might be a pirate, too. . .

In that case, Shark would deal with her as she deserved.

Again the thought occurred to him, irritating and

annoying, that he really needed a vessel of greater force than this present sloop *Draco*. Yes, he would have to do something positive about that. If that vessel out there was a pirate and she was commanded by a piratical captain inimical to Shark—and there were plenty of those sailing the Caribbean—he could be in trouble if he did not watch his seamanship very closely.

If only *Doña Rosaria* had not sunk! If only those fanatical bastards of Spanish had not scuttled her!

Fretting like this would do no good. He went below and paced about the silly cabin, barely avoiding bumping his head, went on deck again for freer air and space, and still that sail hung stubbornly and ominously just above the horizon. Someone over there was keeping an eye on *Draco*. She was no honest merchant, then. More likely a Spanisher. In that case there was only one thing he could do. He gave the necessary orders and *Draco* went on the other tack. It would be dark fairly soon; but there was a moon almost at the full and Shark had no fears of a night encounter.

He went below again and up on deck again, and Pierre eyed him askance. With the instinct that had brought him through a hundred encounters, the captain sensed the wrongness about this situation.

He stood braced, staring ahead, alert and sharp-eyed. As the strange sail bore steadily on on the opposite tack he gave his low-voiced orders, and Barbados Ben at the tiller held and met *Draco* and turned her sweetly so that she was positioned either to fight or to run. Running from an enemy who could blow you out of the water was no cowardice in Captain Shark's book; it was sheer common sense.

Lazarus Wormleigh came aft, touching his forelock. He had learned fast in *Draco*.

"Cap'n," he said in his hoarse voice. He looked excited, swallowing a great deal, quivering. "That's *Venture Lass*!"

Shark was not fool enough to question the identification.

Wormleigh began a tirade of invective. Spittle ran from the sides of his mouth, and he shook his fist wildly at the oncoming vessel.

"*Venture lass*!" he ranted. "As Cap'n Phillpotts was the cap'n of! Now that black bastard Goliath Niven has 'er! Ar! I'd like to draw out his tripes on a wheel, Gord 'elp me!"

In the normal manner of any prudent sea officer seeking information, Shark had already questioned Wormleigh on *Venture Lass's* strength. The main details came through clearly enough.

*Venture Lass* was a low-built, speedy three-master, with twenty-eight guns; eighteen demi-culverins on the main deck, eight sakers on the quarterdeck, and a couple of minions on the poop.

Shark felt no emotions of annoyance, or anger, or despair. This was just one more encounter on the blue Caribbean that had come to nothing. He was completely sure of what he had to do, and he was completely sure his men would not question him.

"Bring her about, Ben," he said, in his low, soft drawl.

"Aye, Cap'n," said Barbados Ben.

Everyone aboard knew that *Venture Lass* would blow *Draco* out of the water, or cut her mast down and then pepper her until she surrendered. After that they'd be butchered. Any attempt to board could be easily thwarted by the superior ship's power and agility and abundance of men.

No longer were they running down to board and

79

plunder; now they were attempting to avoid that fate. There was nothing in this to disturb Shark unduly; he felt tired and he felt a buzzing in his forehead and ears that warned him of possible dire problems to come. He would not think of that now. He would get his sloop out of danger, and then he would think far more seriously about getting command of a force that could take on *Venture Lass* or another of her kind. Had she been Spanish, now, and of three times the strength, why, they'd be in the middle of taking her, right now. . .

As he was thinking those tired thoughts, Isabella was coming to her own decisions.

Down in his tiny great cabin Shark looked up as Pierre came in.

"The Doña Isabella wishes to speak with you, mon capitaine. Of what, she will not say."

"Very good, Pierre. Send her in. Faith! I hope we may come to some understanding about their ransom."

*"Corbleu! Moi aussi!"*

With a fine ironical flourish of his curly feathered hat Pierre ushered Isabella into the aft cabin. She hesitated for a moment. She was well aware of how small and mean a cabin this was, with its plain furniture and low overhead. Compared with the staterooms of the galleons in which she had previously sailed, this cabin was a dismal affair; yet, it seemed large and airy to her when she recalled with a shudder the close confines in which she and the others were being held.

"Come in, señorita, come in. Please sit down."

If he thought to catch her at a disadvantage by his disarming manner and courtesy, he miscalculated. She bore herself with a pride that rose to the occasion. Shark instantly sensed more in this girl than he had expected.

80

For her part, Isabella's heart beat as though it pulsed irregularly at the base of her throat. With the assistance of her maid she had made herself as presentable as possible; she had smoothed the crumples in her gown, tidied her hair, and rubbed her cheeks until they stung so that she might not betray the pallor that this man would know was not the pallor of a highborn lady, but the cheese-skin of fear.

She had come prepared.

So they stood, bent over beneath the overhead, facing each other like two fierce denizens of the jungle, ready to rend the tear—or, perhaps, to indulge in combat no less deadly, if more amusing.

Shark broke that spell.

"Sit down."

She remained standing, and the flutter of her heart beat with a greater pain. "You do not inquire why I came to see you?"

"You wish to discuss the ransom. Aye, you will find me less cordial the longer the negotiations take. That I promise you."

"And I promise you, Captain Shark, that one day they will take you and hang you from the highest yardarm in the fleet—"

"What fleet?" said Captain Shark, crudely.

He moved away in that cramped space so that Isabella could look past him, though the opened horn windows over the tumbling creamy wake of the sloop, darkening now as the quick tropic dusk fell upon the sea, away to the pile of canvas and the heaving bowsprit of another ship—another ship, pursuing this infamous *Draco* of Captain Shark.

Shark saw the abrupt widening of her eyes, the painful flush that stained her cheeks, the quick heaviness of her breathing.

"Aye," he said. He stared at her with that cool

81

detached look that so infuriated women. "Aye. We're running away."

"That ship—"

"He's after our blood, señorita. If he catches us it'll be dancing on air we'll be—"

Isabella could say nothing. A ship was chasing this horrendous pirate. A ship of Spain, hounding down these *corsarios*, bringing her the hope of rescue! This maniac Shark was fleeing, and for all the coolness of him, he must be quaking within his black soul!

Isabella had come prepared; now, with this heaven-sent opportunity, she instantly changed her plans.

"Yes, Captain, I came to talk about ransom. But perhaps that will not be necessary when that galleon catches you."

"She's no galleon—" began Shark.

"What will you think, Captain Shark, when her guns tear your ship to pieces, and destroy your men, and, perhaps, kill or maim you?" She put a hand to her breast. What she intended to do must be done swiftly, or it would not be done at all. "Or, mayhap, Captain, they will slay me."

"They won't do that, señorita."

"Not intentionally, of course not. But by chance." She spoke swiftly, on a shallow breath, and she moved toward Shark. Thinking she wished to look at their pursuer more clearly he moved aside for her, and so she went right aft, and knelt up on the seat to stare out of the pile of canvas and the black hull pursuing them.

A great ship, hungry for the blood of Captain Shark! A ship of Spain, sailing down in might and majesty to redress the wrongs she had suffered, and in doing so to rend and destroy this lean, handsome man with his cool, elegant manners and his ironical detachment, to tear him limb from limb!

Isabella Urraca Castileja de la Cuerva would welcome that, would rejoice in it, would sing praises to the Holy Mother of God!

For some obscure reason in her turmoil of emotions, that thought made her say: "Do you know the name Urraca, Captain?"

Shark looked mildly amused.

"Yes, señorita. It is the old form of Mary."

Isabella was astonished. Few knew what her name meant.

She looked back over the creaming tumbling wake of *Draco* and saw the last low, level rays of the declining sun pitching golden doubloons and ducats into the waves, the blood-red trail stretching far back in the swift passage of this vessel. A chill touched her heart. That great ship following—she would never catch this fleet *corsario*! It seemed to Isabella that a greater distance had opened between the two vessels even in the short space of time she had been in this cabin.

So she must do what she must do.

The idea that she might loosen the upper portion of her gown, sway enticingly towards this Englishman, tempt him, entrap him, smile upward at him and then lower her eyelids, fly all the signals of seduction, all these things occurred to her. But she recoiled. She could not even in this extremity defile herself in that fashion.

She put a hand to her side, and swayed. She let a little fluttering moan slip past her lips.

Shark took a single step towards her, and stopped.

"My lady! You are not well?"

"It is nothing. It will pass."

"By thunder," said Captain Shark. "You give me great cause for concern. I would not wish you to die before I claim the ransom for you."

"Beast!" she said, flaming at him, her color rising now as it willed.

He laughed, and Isabella abruptly pulled her stomach in, so that her small high breasts jutted, and she frowned with such an artistic expression of agony that the gasp she forced out became superfluous.

"Good God!" said Shark. "My lady, you *are* ill!"

He moved toward her as she knelt on the seat and put out his arm. She grasped that arm, feeling through the turmoil of her own thoughts the strong hard purpose of determination in her. His arm was hard and muscular, and she gripped it tenaciously. Shark's other hand reached for her waist to assist her to the cot. She moved with a convulsion of effort like the string of a crossbow twanging forward. She gripped his body with her other hand as he closed with her, and she forced all her strength against her thighs, knees, and legs, and threw herself backward.

*Draco* pitched.

The girl could not have done it alone, her strength could not have matched Shark's strength.

A pitching vessel would not have done it, for Shark lived continually with the movement of ships in great seas.

But the combination proved deadly.

Locked together, the two bodies tumbled through the open window, plunging in a rosette of foam into the wide wastes of the darkling sea.

# CHAPTER EIGHT

Shark took a mouthful of water, and gargled, and got his head above the surface. He bellowed.

"*Draco*! *Draco* ahoy! Ahoy, you deaf useless load of horse manure!"

Then a wave slashed across his face and Isabella dragged him down. There was no time to curse. He put his arms more firmly about her, feeling a small, round softness beneath his palm, hugging her in to him. She did not struggle. She lay close against him, as the seas bore them up and down.

With frightening rapidity the dim bulk of *Draco* passed away below the marching wave crests, and soon only the truck of her single mast showed, yawing and circling against the deepening sky.

Shark rolled himself over, paddling with his feet, his arms wrapped around this stupid bitch of a woman.

Her wet mouth panted against his ear, and water slopped over them, blinding, drenching, battering them in that waste of waters.

"You stupid, silly—" Splash. "—idiot! Numb-skull!"

Isabella felt an enormous strength floating in her

limbs. She was buoyed up. She tasted triumph.

"You are beaten, Captain Shark! Now the Spanish ship will pick us up—and you will hang!"

Shark felt the awful nonsense of the situation slap him with the slapping water.

He spat.

"Spanish ship? What drivel is this?"

"You will scream and pray and beg for mercy, Captain Shark. And you know the mercy we Spanish show to *demonios*!"

"Aye!" They had swung about now, and Shark's finning movements kept their heads above water, so that only the occasional wave broke against them, like the tide bursting against a half-submerged rock. "Aye. You're all foul fiends from the pit. What did you do this for, you stupid bitch?"

"In order to bring you to judgment."

Shark saw it all now, and his curses turned against himself. He had badly misjudged this Isabella Castileja.

"You have brought us to judgment, well enough, if we are picked up."

"The Spanish ship will pick us up, Captain. God will not allow otherwise."

"Mayhap you'll wish He would."

She did not understand him.

"When the Spanish captain knows who you are—"

"What Spanish captain?"

She flailed an arm over her head. Shark looked. *Venture Lass* had seen them. It was quite clear that Captain Goliath Niven had given up hopes of overtaking *Draco*. The head of the frigate turned toward the two in the water. The sails shivered as the yards went over. The last of the sun sinking rapidly into the western horizon painted broad bands of gold and orange across the canvas.

"There, Captain Shark! There!"

"Stupid fool! Idiot! Idle Spanish bitch! That's no Spanish ship. That is a pirate vessel—a *corsario luterano*, a *demonio*, a *ladrón*! That's Cap'n Goliath Niven! He who tears out men's tongues and casts 'em adrift in an open boat! You silly, stupid fool!"

She did not believe.

"You attempt to mock me, to taunt me. I know your filthy sort! When the Spanish hidalgos—"

"There are no Spanish hidalgos aboard that ship—or, if there are, they are wishing they were dead!"

"It is not true—it cannot be—" Now she was unsure. Shark's wildness, she sensed, was not counterfeit.

Shark took a gollop of sea water on his face, and spat, and jerked his fierce head up.

"Look at her flag, while the light lasts."

Isabella looked. She saw. She saw the black flag, and the skeleton, and the English words of fire, death, and destruction. She felt all her limbs dissolving. The power slid down into her bowels and vanished. She screamed, and the seas smashed into her and made her choke and vomit and gag.

"Bloody fool Spanish bitch!"

Isabella shook. Her lips felt numb, like marble lips of a buried statue. "No! It cannot be true. Holy Mary, Mother of God! It cannot—"

"It is, you idiot... They might let me join their merry band. But you—a Spanish lady—Niven'll have you for breakfast."

All her own firm resolve burst forth again.

"No," she said, "No. The Holy Virgin will not condemn me if I drown peacefully, if I sink into the cool green depths away from all pain and suffering. . ."

She forced her arms away, surging back from him, letting herself go. Her head went under. Shark could see her dark hair waving, a darker shadow in the hollows of darkness over the sea.

"No you don't, my girl!" He reached down and seized her hair and dragged her, shrieking and swallowing sea water, back to the surface. He rolled her over, pinioned her arms, and held her up. "I'm not letting you get away with your stupidity so easily! You'd imperil your mortal soul to spite me! But you'll go aboard Goliath Niven's craft and face what ye'll have to face! You'll not spite me!"

As the last pearling drop of blood from the sun coagulated on the far sea rim and vanished, and the world was plunged in darkness, the lady Isabella and Captain Shark were dragged aboard the pirate ship, *Venture Lass*.

Captain Goliath Niven lay in his bunk drunk and helpless. No one would venture to disturb him, for he would as lief lash out with a cutlass, or fire one of his pistols off for the sheer deviltry of it. It had happened before. So the two wrecks of humanity were thrust down onto a small space on the orlop and tied down. The hands that dealt with Isabella fondled her roughly and the men laughed delight-edly as she shrank away. They made very free with her, but they saved her for the captain; for they knew better than to cross Goliath Niven in matters like these.

"Goddamn you for a pack of pesky knaves!" said Shark. "I'm an Englishman! Captain Shark—what the hell are you tying me up for?"

"Jest bide easy, Cap'n," advised a leering fellow with a face filled with pockmarks, a red scarf over his thinning hair, and a gold ring in his ear. "Cap'n Niven'll sort you out come th' mornin'."

"He'll have the hide off you for treating a fellow captain like this!"

"Mebbe he will, and mebbe he won't."

They went away and darkness descended, and Shark was in no mood for polite conversation. Isabella, the horror crawling in her brain and bringing great goose-pimples out upon her skin, lay shuddering, deep sobs tearing her slender form. Shark understood what she was suffering—he wasn't a woman, but he had gone through experiences like this before.

"He'll hold you for ransom, same as me," said Shark, at length. "For God's sake stop crying! You're valuable merchandise."

"Those men—beasts—beasts. . ."

"Aye. Like as not they've been treated as beasts all their lives, by the likes o' you—so I don't blame 'em overmuch. Now get some sleep. It'll be all right in the morning. You'll need your strength to put a brave show on it."

Callous advice, cold comfort. But there was nothing else the captain could give the girl at that time.

The morning dawned fair with the trades picking up as usual as the sun rose. The sea was heaving gently and the swell after the gale was gone. A few clouds fleeced the high sky. Shark and Isabella were brought on deck, where they stood miserably, blinking in the sunlight.

Captain Goliath Niven stalked from his after quarters.

He wore a coat that may have originally been bottle green, but it was now so covered in gold lace that he appeared as a stout, resplendent golden figure. He carried four pistols hanging from a silk sash. His hat perched atop an incongruously huge

89

black peruke. The lace at his wrists and throat showed grubby marks of old grime. At his side swung a massive cutlass, for Niven was not one of your subtle rapier men.

He had a headache. He blinked and cursed and fetched Black Jack a belter across the ear for not getting out of his way in time.

Goliath he was called, but he was not an inch taller than Shark. He was fat, but not uncommonly so in an age of corpulence. Shark suspected he had acquired his name for some other, momentarily concealed, reason.

His finger nails were broken and split, and as black as the chimney flue of the galley.

The pudginess of his face could not conceal the massive jaw which hung, bulldog-like, above his double chin. He shoved his head forward and glared at Shark.

"So you're Cap'n Shark, hey, cully? I've heard tell o' you."

"Good morning, Captain," said Shark. He spoke in his own low musical voice, keeping all rasp of command or authority out of it. This man standing before him, his fat thighs straining at his filthy breeches, pistols and cutlass clanking, the mass of his peruke all greasy, this man was dangerous. His life lay in the man's pudgy hands.

Niven looked at Isabella.

"This is the lady Isabella de la Cuerva," said Shark. "She is worth a very large ransom."

"Shut your mouth, you fancy bastard," said Niven, in high good humor. He walked around Isabella, whose dress, still wet, clung to her. Niven made an admiring circuit.

"A Spanish lady, hey? And worth a ransom, hey?" He threw his heavy head back and guffawed. "Now ain't that nice!"

90

His men, gathered into a circle about him, guffawed in their turn. Shark could see they were a scummy lot, the dregs of men in the sweet trade. Scum, dregs, filth, and detritus of the piratical business. They were men he would scarcely have welcomed aboard his own vessel. Their eyes fixed like sucker fish upon the slender loveliness of Isabella Castileja.

"What d'ye reckon, men?" roared Niven. "She'll fetch a tidy price, eh?"

"Aye, Cap'n," they shouted. "A tidy piece."

Isabella looked at the filthy deck between her naked feet and shivered.

"Let's have a look at her, lads."

"Aye, Cap'n! Aye!"

Eager black-clawed hands reached for Isabella's gown.

She cowered back as the gown was ripped free of her shoulders and arms and dragged down, revealing her white undergarments and her shift, all bedraggled and still damp. The gown was ripped off and flung aside.

Shark looked on impassively. He knew Isabella was worth a good ransom. These black-spawned imps of hell were merely having fun with her. And, if he cared to look closely at it, wasn't what Niven was doing much the same as what he, Captain Sebastian Shark, had done? Niven was employing crude physical means in his torture of this girl, where Shark had used refined means; it all came to the same in the end.

As was usual in these piping days, the men were not interested in seeing a totally naked woman. They ripped the white linen from Isabella's shoulders, breasts, and waist, so that it hung down over her thighs in tatters. They all gazed in great satisfaction upon her nakedness. As for Shark; he

91

looked at the slenderness, the incurve of waist and the beginning outcurve of hip; he looked at her small upturned breasts, and then he looked away. Now the men had had their gaze at her, they'd lock her away and see about getting into communication with her uncle, Don Garcia.

The men remained hushed, gazing upon Isabella's naked defenselessness.

"By the horned imps of hell!" roared Goliath Niven. "She's a wench for the plucking, or my name ain't Goliath!"

The men began to yell then, shouting mouths rounding in sweating faces, craggy teeth, splintered and blackened, fanging those seamed lips. Their eyes lusted. Shark looked quickly back at Niven. Surely the fool wouldn't damage his merchandise?

"Be you a virgin, girl?" demanded Goliath Niven.

Isabella's head shot up and the color flamed into her cheeks. She did not reply.

"D'you hear me, wench? Be you a virgin or bain't you?"

"I am, you foul beast!" said Isabella.

Niven roared. Shark saw Isabella's face, and he looked away.

"You, Tarnation Harry—jist make sure-like, eh, lads?"

There was much merriment and coarse fun as Tarnation Harry, who was a little fellow with a list to larboard and a broken nose badly reset, so that he looked more gargoylish than any church waterspout, rolled up to Isabella. The girl stared sickly at him as he bent and probed. The men holding Isabella craned down to see. Suddenly Isabella choked a stifled cry and her body arched, bending with an abrupt convulsive reaction.

Tarnation Harry swung back.

"Stap me, Cap'n. There be nothin' there. She's no virgin!"

Shark had to look at the girl. She herself could not halt the swift and bitter retort that blurted out.

"I am a virgin! I had an accident when I was little—I fell—"

"Oh, aye!" smirked Goliath Niven. "That's what they all say!"

His men guffawed. They were enjoying this. Some of them were holding their sides as they choked out great whoops of laughter.

"An accident! That's the kinda accident I'd like to have had, swelp me!"

Looking at the great Spanish lady, now a half-naked, defenseless girl ringed by men, Shark suddenly felt he could half-believe her. It was possible. But it was unlikely. Niven wouldn't damage the goods, now. . .

Slowly, Niven began to remove his enormous gold-laced coat, revealing a grimy shirt with the expensive lace ridged and rimed with dirt. "Fetch out a heap o' canvas, an' best sailcloth, lads," he said. "And somethin' soft—we don't want the lady's back skin damaged, now, do we?"

Shark moved forward. He felt again that pain stab down through his head, that old, familiar, hateful pain. He shook that head of his, trying to clear it. He stood before Goliath Niven, and he could feel the trembling in his calves as a great and betraying sin.

"Cap'n Niven" said Shark. "If you damage this girl, the ransom—" He felt with absolute clarity a little imp with a forked tail shove his pitchfork up his forehead, into his brain, and twist it. The masts and yards and sails of the ship swayed—as they always swayed—but this time there were two sets of masts and yards—and there were two Captain Goliath Nivens standing before him, leering.

"You can't hurt this girl, Niven! She's my prisoner, not yours! I'm prepared to give—to share—the ransom with you, but—" Again the pain skewered through his right eyeball, circled in his head, and then lanced into his left eyeball. He could feel the wind on his cheeks—cold, cold. . .

"Sink me for a lubber!" roared Niven. "*Your* ransom!"

"Respect her innocence," said Shark. That sounded nothing short of naively stupid. He tried again. "She's a girl, a lady—she's. . ."

The sky, the deck, the masts and sails, all were dancing and wavering before his gaze. He felt the cold crush down on him, there in the fierce Caribbean sunshine.

"A girl!" bellowed Niven. "She's a wench. An' she's a Spanish wench!"

Niven thrust out his arm, freeing his shirt sleeve with its mass of Mechlin lace. Shark took a gulp of air and fought down for an instant that horrible, clinging, fever malady that would engulf him soon in a thralldom more horrible for its slow inevitable growth. He made a grab at Niven's arm. His fingers felt the muscles, and then he tried to jerk the man off balance and put a knee into his groin.

Nothing of the sort happened.

Goliath bellowed, hauled back, smashed Shark around the head, and drove him to the deck. He kicked him a few times as he lay there. Niven abruptly regained his good humor. He left off kicking Shark and roared to his boatswain.

"Git ropes rigged, Bully! Up from the main yardarm! You know!"

"Aye, Cap'n," shouted Bully. "I knows! I knows!"

"An' the quicker they're rigged, the quicker you c'n take your turn!"

Nothing was more calculated to make the boatswain and his crew slave at the tackle. Shark's senses came back slowly. His wrists and ankles were lashed and he was stripped stark naked. He stood there, held up by two bully-boys, and became aware of Isabella staring at him, her eyes huge. He shook his head in despair.

"Up with him, Bully!"

The men were only too happy to await their consummation for a little sport of this nature. It whetted their appetites. Certainly, Goliath Niven found intense pleasure in watching, as Shark was hauled on a line up to the main yardarm. The line was fastened to his wrists. Another line from the ankle-lashings ran down into the sea, passed under the ship, and was drawn up to the opposite yardarm.

Shark knew what lay in store for him.

The damn fever was raging in him now. His head was on fire. Flames leaped behind his eyes. He was sure the top of his skull had been sawed off and the devil was probably using it to sup blood out of. He hung and dangled in the air, and then Goliath gave the signal.

Shark's body shot down to the sea.

He plunged in bodily.

The rope attached to his ankles pulled him down and under the ship, and dragged him under the keel, and up, and presently hauled him out to dangle upside down from the opposite yardarm, spouting water and blood.

The men gave a cheer when he appeared.

Then the rope attached to his wrists tightened as men hauled on the line on the other side of the ship. Down into the sea once more plunged Shark. He had a moment's clear reflection in the bellowing madness engulfing him to be thankful that *Venture Lass* had been recently careened. Her double-planked bottom was relatively clean. The barnacles that normally festooned a ship's bottom would cut a man to the bone, would flay him, so that instead of hauling a man up to the yardarm, the torturers would haul up a lump of flayed flesh.

Shark dangled from the yardarm, feeling so much pain that nothing remained real or substantial.

"Hold 'im there! Let 'im sweat while I show how it should be done!" Goliath bellowed a huge delighted laugh.

Looking down Shark saw Isabella thrown backwards onto the piles of cloth, saw her shift roughly thrown back up to her waist, and then he could not see her any more for the broad back of Goliath. Shark let out what should have been a strong and powerful yell of anger and condemnation. Only a little whimper whispered past his bruised lips.

When Goliath had finished Isabella lay back, her eyes closed, her mind sharp and contained and filled with an anger that each man merely whetted. For a time between each man Shark was keelhauled. Then Goliath strolled over as Shark once more plunged down, upside-down, toward the sea.

"Avast, you dogs!" bellowed Goliath Niven.

Shark's body hung, his head on a level with the bulwarks. Niven studied him.

"Once more! Once more, just to let him know who's master here. Then take him below. There's a little plan I have for this fine fancy Captain Shark. Handsomely, now!"

Larruping Jake looked up from where he strained over the white body of Isabella, grunting and heaving. "Avast there, Cap'n! Let me finish here before—uh—you keelhaul the bastard—uh—again!"

So Shark hung upside down and watched as Isabella went through her ordeal yet again. Then he was dragged down, through the water, dark and ominous about him, feeling the harsh timbers of the ship bruising and bashing him, feeling the ropes cutting into his wrists. And yet he hardly felt those sensations this time, for they had driven in with agony so many times before that he had come to know each jolt, each barnacle-cut, each horror of that passage beneath the keel of the ship. Half-drowned, bleeding from myriad cuts over his body, bruised and battered, he was drawn in and hurled down onto the deck.

Just before he lapsed into black unconsciousness he saw the long line of men waiting, shifting impatiently, making witty obscene remarks, all waiting their turn.

# CHAPTER NINE

"Don't let him die, Leech, or I'll do the same for you!"

Leech Langford looked up, the fear quick and evident in his eyes. He had a mass of hair over the rear portion of his skull and a massive bald pate forward. His clothes were the remnants of what a ship's surgeon might once have worn. His face, quick and furtive, betrayed the hopelessness of his position.

"He has the fever, Goliath, a bad attack. The keelhauling did him no good—"

"Ha!" shouted Goliath Niven. "I'll wager it did no one any good, by God!"

"But, Goliath, he was like to die before you keelhauled him."

"I don't want any mangy excuses from you, pill-roller! Git him on his feet again! I ain't finished with him yet!"

The orlop was dimly lit by a lantern, and the creak and groan of the ship's timbers resounded together with the swish and wash of the water alongside. The regular banging of wood on wood, the sudden crack as a timber started at each roll and then cracked back, formed a pattern of sounds. Slowly Captain Shark came back to life. He was dreadfully weak; but he would live.

When Leech Langford reported this to Captain Goliath Niven, the pirate grumped with satisfaction.

"You'll not keelhaul him again, Goliath?"

"I might! If I'd a mind to!"

Leech Langford, with the privilege of addressing this monster as Goliath, was not fool enough to contradict Niven. Instead, he said: "He'll need food and rest before you can do anything else to him. He wouldn't know, anyway."

"Aye, Leech. Aye, I know that."

*Venture Lass* sped on across the blue Caribbean with the brilliant sunshine falling everywhere like a promise of heaven; Isabella lay on deck, and whenever a man fancied a little diversion she would find her shift flung back. She had grown used to this by now. She had found a strange new sensation flowing from her, from time to time, when a man was not too quick. She wanted to find this sensation again. When Goliath took her she arched her back, clinging to him, moaning, and he would roar in huge and gratified delight.

One day, in the afternoon, Goliath stormed on deck to order Isabella carried to his cabin. He saw two men fighting. That was unusual. The Articles expressly forbade fighting between the Brethren. Larruping Jake held his knife in his fist and his face was murdering-ugly. Boston Zeke also held his knife, and his face mirrored Jake's.

"I want her, Jake, and I mean to have her!"

"That you don't, Zeke! I'm having her!"

They fought. The knives flashed wickedly, and Jake's knife found Zeke's stomach, and Zeke screamed and pitched forward, spouting blood, dying in his own blood on *Venture Lass*'s deck.

Goliath Niven roared his fury and stormed forward.

Isabella Castileja looked on, and she laughed, high and shrilly.

"Who is going to give it, then, my brave boys?" she called out.

Goliath struck her across the mouth.

"Lay still, you whore! Bully! Seize up Larruping Jake! He's gone done murdered Boston Zeke over the wench!"

"I didn't murder him!" protested Jake, wildly. "'Twas a fair fight, surely!"

All the same, fair fight or not, the Articles saw to it that Larruping Jake was strung up.

That was only the first. More fights broke out around the white and ravished body of Isabella.

At last Niven swore vilely. He gave orders for Isabella to be confined in his own quarters. "Ye starveling wretches! Ye'll get at the wench when I give you leave!"

The pirates were not pleased at this. Ugly rumors began to fly about the frigate. The more Isabella arched her back and clung to him the more Goliath realized the men would no longer tolerate the situation. He would have a mutiny on his hands in no time. Yet he did not want to kill the girl out of hand. He'd kill her, quick, and think no more of it. But. . .

Old Crampton, the sailing master, at last plucked up his courage. He came into the great aft cabin, blinking, touching his chin with fingers that trembled. Goliath was drinking rum, and Isabella was kneeling by his legs, fondling him.

"It can't go on, Cap'n. If you won't share the wench, they're talking of taking her for themselves."

Goliath started up, his anger filling the cabin.

Then he slumped back.

"I know. But I damn well won't give in. I'll see 'em all in hell first!"

"You remember Cap'n Will Phillpotts?"

"I remember, curse you for a whining dog!"

But bluster would not alter the situation.

"A ship's no place for a woman. We've had three murders so far, and more to come, mark my words, Cap'n."

For all his foul temper and bluster Goliath Niven knew how to reckon up the odds. That was how he had come to be elected captain of *Venture Lass*. But he could be deposed. There were plenty of the ship's crew only too willing to chop him down, or stick a knife in his back, or pistol his brains out. The wench was the cause of it. Niven was, as he almost habitually was, on the verge of drunkenness. He could function when other men would be stiff. Now he drank more rum, spilling some so that it rilled down his shirt and drops fell onto the floor. Isabella licked the drops up, eagerly.

"Do with the girl what you plan for Shark, Cap'n. It's the only way."

And, in the fullness of time, Goliath Niven saw that it was, in truth, the only way. Short of killing the girl. He had an idea about that, did Captain Niven. He lusted after her, and she lusted after him—or any man, now she had been well and truly broken in—and he fancied he could get the better of a mangy parcel of dogs like this crew of *Venture Lass*.

The parcel of dogs had other problems.

"We've not sighted a sail since the wench came aboard, Cap'n," grumbled Bully. "She's brought us bad luck."

Others echoed those sentiments.

So it was that, on a fine Caribbean morning, the pinnace was swung out and lowered into the water. Wearing only her tattered shift, the Doña Isabella was handed down into the boat. Shark was driven down at sword point. The crew bent to the oars. Goliath Niven, his sash of pistols across his swag belly, his cutlass tucked up, sat in the sternsheets, his huge hat with its flamboyant feather nodding against sun-glitter on the sea. The oarsmen gave way and the pinnace pulled away from *Venture Lass*.

Shark looked forward with lackluster eyes. He was over the fever, that damned dreaded diabolical fever that would snatch at his robust frame and turn him into a drooling weakling. He had done nothing to help Isabella. That he would have done something, had he been able, still had power to surprise him. The pinnace approached the low coral island with its sandy beach; a few dispirited palm trees drooped, a few sea birds wheeled, calling harshly.

The pinnace grated on sand.

Bound with ropes, Shark was flung out onto the sand. He wore only a pair of breeches. He lay there, winded, feeling the sand in his hair, gritting against his cheek. He saw Isabella brought onto the island, he saw the whole boat's crew use her, and then Goliath Niven—and the way she shrank from them all, writhing, pleading, shrieking.

"Do not leave me! Take me with you! Please, I beg of you!"

"You're too much trouble, wench. Sweet, but poison."

So the pinnace pulled away. They left a breaker of water and a bag of biscuits. That was all.

Shark rolled over and managed to sit up.

The pinnace was lifted from the water and swung inboard. The yards rose, the canvas dropped and was sheeted home, the yards braced around, and with the ever-present trade wind urging her on, *Venture Lass* sailed over the rim of the world.

"Marooned!" said Captain Shark. "Keelhauled, and marooned!"

This was a favorite punishment inflicted by pirates.

They had surely killed both him and the girl. They had marooned them on one of the innumerable little islands or cays, left them there with a mocking token of food and drink, left them to go mad and die of thirst.

Isabella walked over to him. She stood looking down on him.

"Untie the ropes, Isabella, please."

"So you do beg me, now, Captain Shark!"

"I am sorry. It was not my fault you—"

"Why should I untie you? You are a *demonio*."

"You are safe from me, Isabella. I'm just about done for, anyway. That damnable fever—"

"I saw you—before—I saw you when they keelhauled you. You are lucky to be alive."

"Very lucky. *Venture Lass* had been careened recently. And, I confess, I knew little of what was going on. My God! How I ache!"

She stood regarding him, her head on one side.

"Well—will you untie these ropes or not?"

"Why should I?"

Shark groaned and closed his eyes.

"Why, indeed?"

"We will die here, will we not, Captain Shark?"

"It seems very likely."

"Likely?"

"We do not know where we are. But there are trees, there are birds. Much may be done with less."

Her eyes widened. "You think we could escape?"

"If trying will do it, we will escape. But I can do nothing with my hands tied."

"But—"

Shark shook his head and was pleasantly relieved that the ache did not flow at once. He was recovering. Had he been in possession of his full strength he felt he could have snapped these ropes with a single surge of his muscles. But he had tried. And the ropes had groaned and cut into his flesh and had not broken.

Isabella went away and found the water breaker and took out the bung. She lifted it clumsily and tilted it over her mouth and poured. Some of the water went into her mouth. She gulped greedily. Some of the water ran over her chin and down her throat and into the hollow between her breasts.

"You bloody fool!" yelled Shark. "Don't waste the water. It's all we have."

She let the breaker fall to the extent of her arms and, with her head up and the water breaker hanging, she glared at him.

"All *we* have, Captain? *We*?"

"You condemn me to death then?"

Shark opened his mouth and breathed hard, and then shut his mouth. He was feeling the strength coming back, but he was still as weak as a kitten. This Spanish bitch had all the cards in her hand.

"We are both dead, Captain. Both!" She laughed crazily and swung the breaker up with all her strength and hurled it into the sea.

Shark let his breath out.

The wench had gone mad. Well, it was not surprising.

She sauntered over to him. She let her tongue run around her lips, savoring the last of the water drops. She stared with a calculation at this English captain. She had found out things about herself, about her body, over these last days that she had not believed possible. She should have let that fine, swashbuckling Don Mercurio have his way with her, as he had so passionately insisted, when she had the chance.

By the Holy Mother of God! What a fool she had been! The fierce fire in her belly hungered now for what she had lost.

She bent to Shark and probed him.

He gave a grunt of surprise.

"You need not be untied for this, Captain."

"Get away, you whore!" yelled Shark. He felt shattered.

She looked her surprise.

"All men desire—"

"Yes! All men desire. But in their own ways and in their own times. What the hell's happened to you, Isabella?"

She laughed. The laugh cracked flat and ugly over the sandy beach.

"I am become a woman. And I like it. I *like* it, Captain!" She advanced again, kneeling now on the sand. She licked her lips again, and her eyes were bright upon him. "If I untie you, will you—"

"Untie me, and then we may talk."

"It is not talk I want, Captain."

Shark glared at her. He was not baffled. He knew what to do, for this wench was Spanish and therefore outside the pale of civilized behavior. But that was what those dogs of Niven's had thought, there on *Venture Lass*. He could see with an appalled inward clarity what they had done to Isabella. She did not understand. Pity was useless, for she was merely a different kind of woman knowing what she knew now, and the old Isabella was dead. Yet, for all that, Shark could not just blindly repeat the offenses of the pirates. She was Spanish, yes; but she was a human being. That was a novel thought for Captain Sebastian Shark, about anyone Spanish other than Don Jaime.

"Let us talk, then, Isabella. We may not be able to talk when our tongues turn black and stick out of our mouths."

"I may untie you, Shark, if you will promise—"

"You would trust the promise of a *demonio*?"

She sat back on her heels. She had not bothered to draw her tattered shift up over her bared breasts. Now she put her hands to those small firm mounds. "You are a man, Shark, and all men desire all women—"

"Not all men and not all women."

"I do not speak of your buccaneers with peculiar tastes. I speak of *men*!"

Shark deliberately looked away from her. God knew, she was alluring enough. He looked away over the beach and out across the sea, and the courses and topsails struck so brilliantly into his eyes that he blinked. He blinked again. The galleon remained real. It was not a figment of his imagination.

"Isabella," he said, urgently. "There is a ship—"

"Oh, yes, Shark." She was looking at him with a great meaning on her face. "I am sure." She took her hands away from her breasts, and half rose, then lay back. She pulled her shift up her long legs. "Look, Captain Shark. If I untie you all this is yours, Would you not give your immortal soul for this?"

About to blast and blaspheme, Shark saw the only thing to do. The galleon was in fair sight. But

106

unless he made a signal, she would sail on and they would never be picked up.

"Of course, Isabella. You are right." He essayed a smile, which hurt, and went on: "I will do as you desire. Now untie me, and quickly."

"You promise to do as I desire?"

"Yes."

She leaped on him with a deep, throat-filling laugh. The knots came free and the ropes slipped from his wrists. The blood thundered in his veins and he caught the quick groan of agony. There was no time to wait about, suffering. He grabbed Isabella fiercely. She surged up to him so that their bodies met. He broke away, seized the hem of her shift and ripped it away from her naked body.

"What are you doing—?"

Shark ran wildly along the beach, waving the shift over his head. He swung it wildly, this way and that. He did not shout, although the temptation to do so was great. He saved all his breath for running and waving.

Isabella started after him.

She saw the ship.

She stopped stock still.

Then she sank to her knees and buried her face in her hands and sobbed. Her naked shoulders shook with the violence of her sobbing.

The galleon continued serenely on.

She passed beyond the spit of land, and Shark, panting and floundering through the sand, forced his aching body on. He reached the spit and saw that the expanse of water beyond was empty. The galleon had rounded the end of the island. She had sailed away.

"Goddamned useless poxed Spanish lookouts!" said Shark.

Isabella picked herself up and ran fleetly after

Shark. Her naked body flamed in the sunshine.

She forgot her English, such was her passion. She flew along the beach, kicking sand. Shark half-turned and she was upon him.

"You would have called the ship, even though she was Spanish!" she cried. She spoke her native tongue.

"Yes," said Shark, in English. "At least, you would have been saved."

Isabella stepped back, suddenly. Her breasts trembled. She shook. "You speak—"

"Aye. What of that now?"

"But—you must know many—I cannot think—what has been happening?"

She stood there, her whole body trembling. The sun stroked slender golden gleams over her skin. She was white for a Spanish girl, white, smooth, voluptuous. Shark saw her. He saw her as she was, and his mouth went dry.

"You've been living in a nightmare, Isabella. But you must forget that now."

"I—forget?" Her chin lifted. "No, Captain Shark. I do not think I can forget."

"Well," said Shark in his best brutal Captain Shark fashion. "If you cannot forget, then you must learn to live with it."

She scuffed her toe in the sand. "That ship. She flew the flag of Spain, the gold and the red. She was a great galleon. You know what they would do to you—yet you tried to signal them."

"I doubt they'll be worse than the devils in hell." Then he laughed. He laughed, did Captain Shark, there on a desert island, marooned, standing before a gorgeous naked girl. "Faith, though, and I'm wrong in that. You Spanish are a pox worse than all the devils put end to end."

"You hate the Spaniards, Captain. You fear them and hate them."

"Yes, I hate 'em, Isabella. and I fear 'em, too, when they have the upper hand. And—and I despise 'em, the whole godforsaken stinking tribe of 'em."

"You—hate me?"

"Why—" He stopped. How could he hate this poor creature now?

"Why, I do not think I care to discuss that with you. We must find wood, something that will burn, anything. We must make smoke. If I know your oily, poxed Spaniard he'll be so long getting himself off the island he'll surely see the smoke."

"And how will you make fire?"

"Like the Indians. Now do not argue—I've a mind to take my chances with the dons, devils though they be, rather than rot here."

"Then you have your chance."

"The ship is gone. There is no chance here. We must get over to the other side of the island, make smoke—"

"Look, Captain Shark."

Isabella lifted one rounded arm, pointing out to sea. Shark turned. A second great galleon rode in, her hull a blaze of crimson, her sails painted and billowing, her flags, gold and red, flying and fluttering bravely. He saw the rows of gun ports. He saw the wink of steel from her deck.

"No, we will not have to wait." He eyed her. "You asked me if I hated you, Doña Isabella. I do not. God forgive me, I do not hate you."

She smiled. The smile was lazy, sensual, triumphant.

She held out her arms to him.

"Look at me, Shark. Look at my body. My body

knows how to sing new songs, to make new praises on high. Will you join me in a hymn of praise and prayer, body to body?"

Shark waved the shift above his head. It was unnecessary.

The galleon's main course and topsail went to the mast, the lateen slopped over. A boat lowered. He looked at this naked girl, and he knew that for all the lust burning in him, he wanted nothing of her shameless, beautiful, naked, and deadly body.

"The boat is coming, Doña Isabella. They can see us."

He handed her the shift. She took it in fingers that had lost all their tremble. She slipped it on and fiddled with the broken strings, drawing it high about those tender breasts. She looked a different woman now. Where before she had been a brazen, naked sprite, now she was a demure, shipwrecked maiden.

The boat grounded, the oars went up. Men splashed into the shallows. An officer, cocking up his rapier, leaped out and strode ashore. Others followed. They were intrigued, no doubt of that.

Shark met them, coolly, standing straight.

The leading officer half-bowed to Isabella, staring at her in perplexity. He was a handsome young man with a black mustache, no doubt from the best families of Castile.

"I am Isabella Urraca Castileja de la Cuerva!" Isabella said. She made of it a victorious announcement, as though that explained everything. "I was taken from the *Doña Rosaria* by *demonios, ladrónes,* and cast ashore here."

"I thank the Holy Mother of God we have rescued you," said the hidalgo. "Don Hernandez will be overjoyed. Where is the Duchess Marfisa, my lady?"

110

"She is not here. She is with the *corsarios* commanded by Captain Shark."

"Captain Shark!" The officer caught himself. "I am newly from Spain, but I have heard of this *ladrón* Shark."

"You may do more than hear of him, señor. You may take him and lock him in your deepest cell! Here! This is Captain Shark!" Her slender finger pointed unwaveringly at the Captain.

# CHAPTER TEN

Well, of course. He should have known better.

He should have made passionate love to Isabella, there on the sand of the desert isle. He should have sworn eternal love, undying fidelity, anything. She now knew he could speak Spanish; with his knowledge he could have passed easily for a Spaniard, of any estate. He could have done it—he had done it.

Why, then, had he drawn back?

Next time, Shark vowed, as he lay fettered and manacled and in the bilboes in a stinking hole of the orlop, next time he would not be so squeamish.

But something about the girl, her naked body, her tiny breasts, her haughty airs, the sensual furnace bursting up through every pore, something about her had revolted him. Next time, perhaps; but Sebastian Shark knew he could have done no other than he had done with Isabella Castileja.

Anyway, more than one of Goliath Niven's crew was poxed to the eyeballs. Shark did not believe in going into hazardous encounters of that nature.

The Spanish did feed him, on the journey back to San Isidro, on slops and foulnesses he wolfed down with a strong stomach. They gave him as many cuffs and kicks as food; but Shark bore them all and stored them away in his memory.

Shark's memories wended back, back to Algiers, back to old Abd al-Rahim—the Slave of the Compassionate—whose marvelous and magical skills of medicine had brought Shark through bouts of illness that would have killed a man suffering under Western doctors and leeches. There is no way of saying a simple, plain, straightforward "thank you" in Arabic, so Shark had blessed Abd al-Rahim and prayed his shadow would never grow less, that Allah would increase his weal, and so on and on. When that damned diabolical fever struck him, as it was wont to do from time to time, he would wish for nothing else but that old Abd al-Rahim should appear at his side, with his white hair, and his seamed, benign face, and those fingers so touched with tender magic.

His own turbulent life had given Sebastian a barnacled growth of calluses, proof against most adversity; or, at the least, giving him the courage and stoicism to outface miserable fate. He had been captured by the Spanish. They would be monstrously unkind to him. This prospect did not please him, but it did not daunt him. Faith! If he couldn't smash a few Spanishers' faces in, and degut a few more, and snatch up weapons and escape, his name wasn't Captain Sebastian Shark!

Don Pedro and Perlita were at it again. A fresh consignment of victims for the torture dungeons had been brought in, and Don Pedro had grown quite excited.

He had watched a stout Dutchman having his legs crushed. The way the bones had splintered, jagging bloodily through the man's flesh and skin, and the

113

sounds—ah, the sounds!—had brought a flush to his fat cheek and a quiver to his loins. He had trotted up the curving stairs, sweating and panting, and Perlita had, as always, been ready.

"You are a bull, Don Pedro," said Perlita, giggling. She had this familiarity with him in private, of course; absolute and iron submission to the rules of subservience were observed outside his private suite. "You great stallion."

She knew how to please the old fool. He panted and thrust; then the smacking crack of the signal gun brought him up, red-faced, with the sweat running down his sagging cheeks and his mouth open. He thrust his body up on both arms, straight, and look upward.

"Now by all the devils in hell!"

Perlita sighed. She wiggled. But Don Pedro was too well aware of what the signal gun portended to waste any more time trying to resuscitate a fallen cause.

"Don Hernandez," he groaned. He clambered off Perlita and stood up, feeling the shake in his legs.

As she helped him to dress, Perlita made soothing little sounds and rubbed herself against Don Pedro, but the signal gun had fired and the passion had ebbed. When at last Don Pedro was fully dressed, with his peruke listing just a little to starboard, he took his cane, his laced kerchief, his snuff box, and so accoutred for the coming confrontation, he descended from his villa to greet the incoming ships.

His thoughts would not allow him to believe they had found his cousin, the Duchess Marfisa. His fat face wrinkled up in calculation. The problem would be to prove she was truly dead. The laws were strict. He was an "old Christian." *Limieza*—purity of blood—was firmly established in the family. He was not aware of any *conversos* or *marranos* among his own entourage. Had he found any of these people, who professed good Catholicism but whose parents or ancestors had been Moors or Jews, he would have got rid of them at once. He suspected that the inquisitor, Father Dominic, that blade of remorseless steel in Don Hernandez's suite, would do the same. So if Marfisa could be proved dead, and everyone else who would want a finger in her money could be disposed of, Don Pedro should come handsomely out of this. He felt the smirk on his face was entirely warranted.

As usual everyone turned out to watch the ship come in.

Flags fluttered, the sun shone down, street vendors cried their oranges, water, and sweetmeats, dogs ran yelping, and everyone looked forward to a good time when the sailors and soldiers came ashore.

The ship rounded the stone castle on its point and lay grandly for the harbor. She was Don Hernandez's flagship, *Nuestra Señora del Rosario*, and she was, in truth, a fine grand galleon, built after the more advanced style that lent less weight to tallness and number of decks and more to speed, maneuverability, and an armament of homogenous power. Gone were the days of a bewildering multiplicity of different sizes of guns on a raking gallery of decks and half decks.

"A grand sight, Don Pedro!" said Don Garcia, limping up. The ribbons on his cane were brilliant in the sunshine.

"A good ship, Don Garcia. I trust she will bring good news." Don Pedro meant, of course, good news for Don Garcia about his niece Isabella Castileja. He would far prefer Don Hernandez, Marquis of Requanza, to bring no news of Marfisa—

or, best of all, positive news of her demise.

"The marquis sails alone, I perceive."

"No doubt the other ships of the squadron will follow shortly."

*Nuestra Señora del Rosario* moved splendidly into the harbor of San Isidro. Guns boomed sonorous salutes and the white smoke puffed. She let her topsails fly in a pretty gesture that added to the excitement on shore. Men were to be seen pouring up the shrouds and working their way out on the yards. Topsails and courses disappeared, the lateen mizzen vanished, not without a number of obstinate flappings and bangings, and the sprit sail likewise was furled, as the ship's anchor let go with a roar and a splash. Don Garcia had seen these sights many times, and he sighed, and felt his old wound itching him, so that he balanced more heavily on his cane.

"Would we had a fleet of such ships," he said, with the fierce pride burning in him.

"We had three here a short time ago," Don Pedro could not stop himself from saying, darkly. "I pray the Holy Virgin we still have them."

*"Nuestra Señora del Rosario* is a modern ship, Don Pedro. I am convinced the *corsarios* have nothing to match her strength. She mounts twenty-four guns on her gundeck, and each one is a mediocañon. And on her upper deck she carries twenty-four of the extraordinary new *medioculebrinas.*" Don Garcia waxed enthusiastic on his pet subject of ships to beat the Egnlish. Most of the hidalgos merely required a ship to be driven at the enemy so that they might board her and fight as the good God intended man to fight, on his own two legs. Don Pedro was aware of this odd interest of Don Garcia's, and for the sake of harmony he did not criticize. "Also," went on Don Garcia,

staring with a hollow, sick longing at the ship, "she has six sakers on the quarterdeck, besides murdering pieces and—"

"Yes, yes," interrupted Don Pedro, a thing a governor might do, with suitable care and show of warm friendship. "But here is Don Hernandez."

The marquis stepped ashore in high good humor. He had not yet succeeded in rescuing the Duchess Marfisa, but he had news of her, and he had captured a raggle-tailed parcel of cutthroat *corsarios luteranos*. He would extract further information from them, with the timely assistance of Father Dominic. Yes, considered Don Hernandez, as he stepped with youthful vigor towards the two hidalgos waiting to receive him, things were progressing well for him in his mission to New Spain, and it could only be a matter of time before he had the Duchess Marfisa safely restored—and panting in his passionate arms, as he phrased it, with a sly nod toward the fiery poets of Old Spain.

The three men stood talking for a space, as the marquis explained that he had been separated from his two consorts. He had no fears for them. Although neither was a fine nor formidable a vessel as his beautiful *Nuestra Señora del Rosario*, they were still powerful fighting ships.

"Why, señores! we merely fired a broadside at this miserable English corsair and she surrendered meekly, without firing a shot."

"That is indeed brave news, Don Hernandez. And the news of my cousin?"

"The news of my niece, Don Hernandez?"

"As to the Doña Isabella, Don Garcia, I have nothing to report to you, an unhappy state of affairs and one which I trust the saints will quickly rectify. But these *corsarios* tell me that the duchess is safe and unharmed, and that a ransom demand will soon reach us. She has been taken, I understand, by a certain Captain Shark."

Don Garcia licked his lips. He saw through the marquis swiftly.

"You do not tell me all, Marquis."

"Surely you do not doubt Don Hernandez, Don Garcia?" Don Pedro looked aghast. This could be serious.

"I do not doubt his honor. I am strong enough to be told the truth!"

Don Hernandez had heard of the heights to which Don Garcia ascribed his honor. The man was a fanatic on the subject. His hot blood would never overlook a slight. The smallest stain on his honor, or the honor of his family, would be wiped out in blood.

"It grieves me, Don Garcia, to have to tell you my news. I was hoping—but I see it would be a cruelty to withhold it from you."

"Yes, Don Hernandez. You have ill news of Isabella?"

"The worst, I believe. She and this infamous Shark were lost overboard from the *demonios'* ship. They were lost, it is certain."

Don Garcia lifted his chin. His wrinkled and veinous hand gripped the jeweled hilt of his rapier. He walked with a firm stride to his limp, and yet he felt as though he had been beaten all over. "At least," he said with that savage Spanish pride, "at least she took this monster with her to death!"

"Yes, Don Garcia."

"That is what we Castilejas are like! We are confident in our pride, pure in our honor! Isabella merely proved yet again the honor of our family!"

"It seems from what these English tell me that

you are indisputably right. They had the news from Shark's ship. This mad English dog and Isabella were alone in his cabin. When, later, they were missed, the whole vessel was searched. They were not aboard. I think, Don Garcia, your niece worthily upheld the honor of the Castilejas!"

"I give thanks to the Holy Mother of God!"

Don Pedro, whose concern over his cousin had quickly evaporated, shifted anxiously to get to the most important item of news Don Hernandez had brought back.

"And these English prisoners, Marquis? You will have them brought ashore so they may be questioned?"

"Assuredly, Don Pedro." The marquis had already heard about Don Pedro's dungeons. He smiled. "I believe you will find Father Dominic most able to conduct the inquiry."

Don Pedro's fat face shone with sweat. He waddled as he walked. He felt elated. A whole shipload of English *ladrónes* to put to the question! How Perlita would love him!

When the prisoners were brought ashore, Don Pedro found himself a comfortable vantage point from which to watch them being brought into the cells beneath the fort. He sat twitching with pleasure.

The English marched along the stone-flagged courtyard and through the iron-barred portals and past the thrown-back iron-studded doors, down and down into the noxious cells. From those cells they would be dragged into the dungeons and the torture chambers.

They were half-naked, in chains, dragging themselves along—and yet they marched. Some were wounded. Two were carried by their comrades.

There were twenty of them. Don Pedro felt a trifle cheated.

"Twenty?" He said to Don Hernandez, who was delivering the prisoners over personally. "That is all?"

"Their vessel was not large, Don Pedro."

"And they struck without a fight?"

"Yes."

Don Pedro thought of all those guns in *Nuestra Señora del Rosario*, and he almost said: "You would not have needed to fire all your broadside to have killed each one separately." However, he did not say this. He disliked bloodshed when it was his own.

He marked one of the prisoners, a very tall lean man who walked with a stoop, and whose naked sides showed his ribs in etched sharpness. His white hair hung lankly. He tried to hold his narrow shoulders back, and succeeded only in accentuating his lower ribcage over a hollow belly.

Another prisoner Don Pedro marked as offering more sport. He wore a patch over one eye. His thick black hair hung down, chopped across his forehead. He hobbled along on one leg, and the breeches laces of the other flapped emptily. He supported himself on a crude crutch under his left armpit, and his round, good-humored face wore a look that Don Pedro could not rightly fathom. This pirate's hands flashed with a multiplicity of rings.

"If Lorenzo can't get those rings off easily, Don Hernandez, that fellow is likely to have stump arms as he has a stump left leg!"

"He had a wooden leg," said the Marquis. "But our broadside sent a roundshot that knocked it away in splinters."

Both men considered that a capital jest.

120

The last prisoner—a mere lad whose lips were dragged inward over his teeth and whose jaws clamped down so that his maxillary muscles stood forth, rigid and white—passed down into the dungeon cells. Don Pedro looked about.

"Which one was the captain?"

"They will not say, I believe he is there, hiding among his fellows. We will find him, never fear."

"I know you bring word that Captain Shark is dead, and I am heartily glad of that. I have had no dealings with him, but of his fearsome character I know full well—"

"I would not use the word character of so foul a creature in God's sight."

"Amen to that, Don Hernandez. But I would not put it past Shark to be among those men. It is possible."

"Aye, it is possible. But he is not. He is dead with Doña Isabella Castileja."

Father Dominic had been well trained. There had been much friction between Spain and the Papacy over the preeminence of the Inquisition, and now Spain's own Inquisition operated as the most powerful organ of the state. Father Dominic acknowledged no masters but the masters of his own order. He moved forward, his hands tucked neatly into the sleeves of his habit.

"I will select two to begin with," Dominic said in his harsh, yet evenly modulated voice. "We must find out their associates. There can be no recantation for them, they are doomed men. But they will tell us what we must know before they die."

Don Pedro nodded, a little uncertainly. This was not quite the same route as Father Jacinto adopted.

They went down into the dripping depths of the

dungeons. Don Pedro found his breath coming faster, his eyes brightened, and he licked his lips. Father Dominic glanced at the hidalgo.

"You may go, señor, if you wish."

"Go! It is my duty to stay, Father!"

Father Dominic let his cynical, worldly smile glimmer on that pallid face, and he wiped his dripping nose.

The first two wretches were dragged into the torture chamber. One was a squint-eyed fellow, robust, with a straggly fair beard, and he struggled futilely until a buffet from one of Lorenzo's assistants quieted him. He was hung up.

The other was the one-legged man with the black eyepatch. Lorenzo looked at his hands, then back to Don Pedro. At a short nod, Lorenzo began pulling rings off.

"Goddamn you for a bunch of papist bastards!" roared the one-legged man. He was short, and would have a paunch if he ate too much. He did not struggle but, with a sudden swiftly cunning movement, rested all his weight on his crutch and shot out his right foot. The big toe smacked into Lorenzo's groin.

Lorenzo fell down. He yelled, and his face turned the color of a bruised plum.

"And I hope you never recover, you whoreson Spanish pimp!"

Assistants hurled the one-legged man down, and his crutch was snatched up and broken across in a frenzied movement of petty revenge. A boot cracked into his ribs.

"Ar! Lancelot James knows your sort o' bully-boys! He's a-met your likes afore!"

"Lancelot James," said Don Hernandez. "Write that down, Leon," to his personal clerk who held

122

writing materials in hands that trembled. By the light of wall torches the clerk wrote down all that was uttered by the prisoners. James lay on the floor, trying to avoid the blows and kicks.

"Enough!" said Don Pedro. "Take him back to the cells. I think I would wish him to be brought back when Lorenzo recovers." He tittered. "It will be instructive to observe how Lorenzo evens the score."

Lancelot James was hauled to his one foot. He balanced on a torturer's arm. He spat at Father Dominic.

"I know you, you black heathen crow! Lancelot James knows your sort, too! You love to see honest men broken! You stinking heap o' horse manure! If'n I had two trotters instead o' one I'd kick your backside into your foreside, you poxy papist piss-pot!"

Father Dominic merely allowed that frozen smile to stay upon his face, and he did not take his hands from the sleeve of his robe. "Take him back to the cells," he said, mildly. "The man speaks Spanish and therefore will be more useful when he has seen some of his fellow *demonios* undergo the question. He will be more amenable then."

"Never for th' likes o' you! Lancelot James spits on you. Ar! He knows a thing or three, does old Lance James!"

The man hanging in chains on the wall regained consciousness, and the questioning proceeded. Presently Don Hernandez excused himself. Don Pedro was barely civil to the marquis as he left. Don Pedro's eyes devoured the blood and the breaking bones, and Don Pedro's ears sang sweetly with the tortured screams. He sniffed the scent of blood.

"Yes, yes, Don Hernandez. I will be with you

shortly. But we must discover who is the captain, must we not?"

Just before the prisoner died—his name was Jack Jones and he was a Welshman—they understood that the captain of this band had been sailing another ship when their little vessel, the *Pope's Flea*, had been taken.

They did not refer to the name of the vessel again.

Leaving his men to clean up and taking only the most necessary polite farewell of Father Dominic, Don Pedro dashed as fast as he could up the curving stairs and in through his secret door. Perlita was waiting. He had sent instructions by Valence to that effect.

Don Pedro ran in, throwing off his baldric and his coat, hurling his hat and peruke to the floor. He stared at Perlita on the wide bed for a moment and she laughed and threw herself backward with a great rustling of petticoats.

"Hurry, hurry, Don Pedro!"

"Oh, oh, Perlita! It was glorious! And I am glorious! I am superb!" With a breaking of points and a slithering of costly taffetas his breeches were down and he was flinging himself on the bed. "Perlita! I am strong, strong!"

"Don Pedro! Oh! Such a man—"

The harshly flat smack of the signal gun cracked through the warm air.

Don Pedro looked up.

His face strained with disbelief.

"Quick, Don Pedro, quick—quick!"

"I—do not—believe it!"

"Oh, Don Pedro! Quickly—Oh! You are going! Going!"

Don Pedro rolled off and sat on the edge of the

bed. He looked down. That infernal gun always fired just when he was about to do the same thing. There must be a plot against him! That fat cow of a wife of his must have bribed a gunner on the ramparts!

He breathed heavily. His calves shook. He got up and found a fresh pair of breeches of yellow taffeta, and struggled into them with Perlita's help. She helped him on with his coat over his flowered vest, his baldric, his vast peruke, and his hat, for which she had to scrabble on her hands and knees, bottom upended, under a side-cupboard. Don Pedro watched, sighed, took the proffered hat, and clapped it on his peruke. His cane, his snuff-box, his kerchief. He pivoted slowly and Perlita studied him, her head on one side.

"Truly, Don Pedro, you are a very great man!"

He couldn't answer that one.

He went out again and met with Don Hernandez and Don Garcia. They watched as the two other ships of the marquis' squadron sailed in.

The news they brought set everything quiveringly alive again.

Such news!

Don Garcia ran limping and hobbling and skipping. He caught up the slender form of Isabella in his arms and hugged and kissed her. She was found in the ship, dressed in a poor dress that belonged to a soldier's dead wife.

"You are safe, *querida*, safe! And you are unharmed! They—they did not harm you?"

"Oh, uncle! I give thanks to the Holy Mother of God I am safe. . .of course not, how could they harm me?"

But Don Pedro and Don Hernandez were staring with a sharp, lusting look upon the lean, tall man who stood upon the jetty. His arms were bound behind his back with manacles, his ankles were fettered, and chains festooned his body. They had been told who he was. They rejoiced. There would be a thanksgiving service in the cathedral. Masses would be sung, and candles lit, and the bells would ring.

Everyone in San Isidro would rejoice.

For Captain Sebastian Shark had been captured!

He was here, safely in Spanish hands, and the Spanish knew exactly what to do.

Captain Shark.

Captured.

Captain Shark, prisoner, soon to taste of the joys of the dungeons and to appreciate the skill of the Holy Inquisition.

Captain Shark.

Prisoner!

Now praise be to Heaven! The holy hour of reckoning was at hand, the Day of Judgment and of Atonement was come!

## CHAPTER ELEVEN

"Shiver me timbers, Cap'n! 'Tis a sorry day they've taken you!"

"And I'm equally grieved to see you here, Lance."

"Ar! Old Lance James knows a thing or three about poxy Spanish jails! We'll get out, Cap'n. We'll bash the black teeth down the fanged wine-spouts o' these poxy-faced guards, and we'll have a rare old skip-to-me-loo up them stairs! Aye, Cap'n! Betwixt Cap'n Shark an' old Lance James, we bonny lads will soon win free!"

"Aye, Cap'n!" and "Aye, Lance!" sounded from the other eighteen prisoners.

The lad unstoppered his lips to shout with them, and as quickly clamped his teeth into his lips again so they drew blood. He was Johnny Chance, and he was eighteen.

"What's the plan, Cap'n?" said Bones. His perpetual stoop and the lean cadaverous nature of his frame made men think he was frail and without strength. Bones could bend an iron bar that far tougher looking individuals could not even put a kink into. His white hair was a memento of a previous sojourn in just such a place as this.

"Afore you tells us th' plan, Cap'n," put in James, "old Lance James thinks as how you oughtta know they're taking us outta here two by two." His face, with its still-smooth outlines, shone with sweat and caked grime, like them all. . . ."I put me toe into the private's o' th' chief torturer. A nasty poxy creature as ever the devil made."

One or two others let out grim cackles at this.

"But he'll have it in for old Lance. Ar! Lance knows an evil sot like that when he sees one."

"They're all a parcel o' fanatics." Shark felt a strange and unreasoning lightening of his spirits. Here he was, fettered, manacled, chained, flung down in filth into a dank and horrible dungeon where the only light came from a torch bracketed to the wall outside the iron bars, and yet he felt freer than he had since the moment that stupid bitch Isabella had pitched him into the wake of *Draco*. She was stupid, but he could find a place for her in that all-encompassing pity for humanity that served him in lieu of any closer personal intimacy.

He was with good, honest Englishmen again. He knew some of them. They were buccaneers, like himself, and some had sailed with him and Captain Elizabeth Wren on earlier cruises. In their little cockle-boat *Pope's Flea* they had been on an errand for Beth Wren and had spoken Shark's *Draco* on the morning of his inexplicable disappearance. From when Lancelot James said, Shark's men—Pierre and Simon and Ned and John and all the others—had been completely shattered by his presumed death. *Draco*, James said, had been like a death ship.

"They'll get over it," said Shark, with a harshness he made no effort to control. "Give them a fat Spanisher to loot and they'll feel fine again."

Lancelot James shook his head. "Old Lance

James ain't so sure o' that, Cap'n. There be only one Cap'n Shark on th' Main, an' everyone who is anyone knows that, glory be!"

Captain Elizabeth Wren had nominated Chalky White, a ferocious fighter, to command the tiny *Pope's Flea* and poor Chalky had had his head blown off by the broadside from Don Hernandez. As James said: "We're keeping the filthy dons guessing as to who's th' cap'n. That way the pizzpots will seek for that answer before they get onto important things."

Shark nodded. You used any weapons that came to hand dealing with the caballeros of Spain. . .

If a man questioned this character, Lancelot James, on the loss of his left leg, he would lay a finger alongside his nose, beneath his missing left eye, and wink his right. "Ar!" he would say. "Old Lance James fair put his foot in it that time, to be sure!"

James had been chief gunner with old Lionel Wells, a great-hearted villain who could cut you a gold purse-string or take his ship under full sail into the mouths of a Spanish battery. During one action, as James and his cronies told it, James, as gunner, had been bringing up fresh powder from the magazine. It seemed a crack or a hole had opened and the powder had trickled out, all unbeknownst to two-legged Lancelot James as he carried it up, trickling down into the boot of his left leg. He'd felt the gritty irritation after a time and had sat on the deck and taken his boot off—and then the Spanish galleon hove up and it was "Hands to Action Stations," and all a rush and a bustle, for the Spanisher showed fight.

"Ar," said Lancelot James, rubbing his nose. "Ar! Old Lancelot James was a fair plucked 'un, in them days. That Spanisher weren't gettin' away from him, lads, eh?"

So he'd jumped up as the first shots crashed in, for the Spanisher had come on them suddenly around a point, and the battle was joined at almost point-blank range. The carcasses had come spitting and smoking in, iron cages stuffed with combustibles, horrible weapons, with hooked chains to grapple rigging and burn the ship. Lancelot James had hopped and skipped to his guns, bawling to his gun crews, still holding his left boot. He had not, of course, seen the chunk of match that had dropped into the boot.

As he said: "Ar! Old Lance James, he was a-yelling to th' lads to point their guns and to fire, and a-trying to pull his boot on. Old Terence, he yelled. "Don't put your boot on, Lance!" he shouted at poor old Lance. But the damned dons was a-shooting and old Lance, he wanted to get into th' fight, and he cussed and blasted the dons, an' he didn't know what th' tarnation hell Terence was a-talking of. "Don't pull your boot on, Lance!" yelled Terence. "You'll be sorry!"

"Ar!" Lancelot James rubbed his nose reflectively. "Ar, Cap'n lad! Old Lance James he pulled his boot on—and—"

"And?"

"And poor old Lance James, he didn't have a leg to stand on."

"Oh."

And someone would always say: "And how come you lost your eyeball, then, Lance, eh?"

"Ar, lad! That's another story!"

Now, here in the dungeons of the fortress of San Isidro, Captain Shark knew he would have to find a crutch, and a wooden leg or something similar, for

Lancelot James. He wouldn't leave the gunner. The men were a parcel of fine desperadoes, and he felt confident that, once they were beyond the bars and grasped weapons in their fists, they stood a good chance of breaking out. The plan would have to be simple. Simple plans more often succeeded. Although, to be fair, Shark had worked his share of complicated and fanciful plans in his time, and he knew he would do so again in the future.

There were twenty of them, still—or nineteen and a half, if you liked.

"Hairy Joes," said Shark. "You and Bilboes Billy stand by th' bars. Lance—you writhe on the floor. Rub some of this nitre from the walls around your mouth—do the foaming bit."

"Old Lancelot James, he can foam and rave with th' best o' 'em, Cap'n lad!"

Shark positioned the others. For Bones he reserved a special duty that might not be necessary.

When he felt confident Shark took a deep breath.

He looked about at his gang of cutthroats, seeing their fierce predatory faces in the flickering torchlight, their eyes gleaming ferally at him. They held themselves ready for whatever deviltry might come.

"Right, lads. The Spanish dogs aren't fool enough to entrust the keys to the outer gates to the jailers who visit us. We can force them to open these gates, but once we are past these bars it'll all have to be done again."

"Aye, Cap'n," they growled. "The Spanish monkeys'll be only too glad to open the gates time we're a-done with 'em!"

The drill was for the jailers to open the barred gateway and to allow a couple of serving men—black men who were so silly with fear they made no difference—to enter the cells with the platters of

131

gunk and pitchers of scummy water. The jailers stayed outside, their weapons ready.

When the corridor lighted with the approach of torches, and when the shuffle of men's feet, the clink of pewter platters, and the indistinct mutter of men's voices penetrated down to the dungeons, Shark put a hand to his lips, gazing on these men with a fierce pride.

The key screeched in the lock, uneasily, and the barred gates swung open. Three black men entered bringing the food. Hairy Joes and Bilboes Billy made no move. Shark looked at the four guards outside, three of them holding torches which shone on their old-fashioned breastplates and morions, for the Spanish here had not yet adopted the new mode of dressing soldiers. He saw the fourth, the petty officer in charge, and noted the puffiness of his eyes, the paunch, the seedy look of him, and guessed he was newly risen from a fever bed.

Shark rubbed his nose.

Instantly Lancelot James crashed to the floor, an easy business for him, and began flailing his arms and one leg. Spittle drooled from his drawn back lips, mixed with the nitre scraped from the walls. Lancelot James spat and frothed and foamed. He did a magnificent job.

Shark leaped forward.

"Don't touch him! Keep clear! 'Tis the plague, sure it is!"

The three blacks did not understand his English, but they understood his meaning. They squalled in terror and bolted for the gate. The petty officer stepped forward, drawing his sword. It was a brass-hilted hanger, a crude weapon, but Shark coveted it down there in the dungeons of San Isidro.

"The plague, you dolts!" he shouted in Spanish.

"Keep clear of him, *estupidos*!"

The petty officer checked and the blacks crashed into him. Then Shark was on him, one hand around his throat, the other raking for the hilt of the sword.

Hairy Joes and Bilboes Billy catapulted past and took two of the guards over as they smashed to the floor. The fourth stood frozen for an instant—then Captain Shark reared up, the hanger a brand of living fire in his fist, and the fourth guard went down. The three blacks were quietly put to sleep, to awake later with headaches and with a mortal terror of English *demonios* indelibly impressed on them.

The four Spanish guards were dead.

Shark sighed.

"They're only poor devils, serving brutal and evil masters. It was the will of God, I believe, for I would not have slain them all."

"Good riddance," said Bones. His specialty had not been needed, and he was baffled and annoyed on that account.

The buccaneers padded cautiously along the corridor. They held what weapons the guards had provided. Hairy Joes and Jake the One supported Lancelot James, and he alternately blessed them for true-blue shipmates and cursed them for his own dependence on them. The torchlight splashed lurid glitters of color ahead, and the shadows writhed and leered from the greenly slimed walls and roof. They pressed on.

"Shet your mouth, timber-toes," rumbled Hairy Joes.

"Shiver me timbers!" bayed Lancelot James. "It's a mortal pity I can't kick your backside for you, Hairy Joes!"

"Quiet back there!" said Shark.

Instantly—silence.

They found and disposed of five more guards as they prowled on, dark and silent and feral. Now they had more weapons. The corridors branched bewilderingly, but Shark marched on unhesitatingly. He followed every upward set of stairs, and took alternate branchings. Eventually they came to a stone corridor of loftier size, with torches becketed to the stone walls, and no greenly dripping fungus upon the stone roof.

"We're high enough up to try for a door." Shark looked at his bedraggled company. Sea wolves, they were called, vermin of the oceans. Well, they would do a little biting before they were through.

The doorway had been closed and bolted, and iron bars in iron brackets sealed it from ingress. From an open door in the side wall came the merry sounds of drinking, and the clicking-clatter of dice being shaken in a cup. Shark pressed against the wall and sidled close.

According to his calculations they should be breaking out just as the sun sank—either just before or just after. No one cast down into those stifling and gloomy dungeons could expect to keep the most accurate count of time without sight of the sun and in the absence of accurate measurements.

Shark moved cautiously, sidling along the wall, his back pressed against the stone. He held the hanger downward in his right fist. Following him came Bones, bearing another hanger, and after him Bilboes Billy and Hairy Joes. Lancelot James had been tucked up against the wall with a pistol. Lance James seldom missed his aim.

Shadows moved across the threshold of the guardroom and a thick voice called out: "Where are

134

the lazy dogs! That Alfonso, I'll—"

"Don't waste time on the *hijo de puta,*" roughly counseled another voice. "Drink up!"

Shark had no way of knowing just how many men were in there, or how many would be looking at the doorway. The situation appealed to the captain. He hawked and spat—loudly.

"*Madre de dios!*" he said in his hidalgo's Castilian. "*Asno! Con prisa!* Out! Out! Is this the siesta? Form up or I'll squeeze your *cojones* under a guntruck! *Vamos!*"

Uproar. Men shouting and stampeding for the door. Clink and clatter of snatched-up weapons. A petty officer shouted something about being on duty "on the double, el capitan." Then the first Spaniard skidded out the door, still trying to get the strap of his morion over his chin.

Shark clouted him behind the ear and Bones snatched him away. Two more followed and were similarly dealt with. The fourth tried to backpedal, but he was knocked forward by the following rush and sprawled out over the flagstones.

The next one staggered, then tripped, his morion toppling over his eyes, his knees buckling.

Shark left these two. By now someone in there must have figured out what was going on. If he stuck his head around the door now, a pistol would bang and his head would splash.

He dropped to one knee and scooped the blade from the scabbard of the nearest fallen soldier. The captain was scarcely thinking now. His calculations were all made; he was acting by bodily reflex alone. He threw himself forward, low, into the door.

A petty officer who was grasping his musket let the thing off with an almighty roar. Smoke gushed, choking. But he had fired waist-high. Then Shark threw his blade, overarm. The steel flew to its target, transfixing the petty officer's throat.

"In!" roared Shark.

He barely had time to get himself up and his hanger into action before Bones and Hairy Joes and the others were trampling through, and they would have trampled all over him in their eagerness. They belted into the rest of the guard. Against devils like this, all hairy and whiskered, with gaunt bodies and blackened faces, with fierce frenetic movements of evil intent, the Spanish soldiers quickly succumbed.

"My oath, Cap'n," said Hairy Joes, scratching himself with his thumb. That hand held the sword, and the tip sprayed blood as Hairy Joes scratched. "My oath! That were pretty!"

"It'll be prettier still when we're outta here! Take what you want, lads, and then to open the door! *Move!*"

That musket shot would rouse the fortress. The buccaneers needed no instruction in how to strip a dead man. They needed no manual of looting. They had what they required bundled and the iron bars taken down and the gates thrown open in the time it took to swig a hefty slug of rum.

Like the prowling wolves for whom they were named, they stole from the gateway. The sun was almost down. Long shadows lay across the moat and the bridge. The fortress towered above them, harsh and massive, serried in rank after rank of tiered battlements. The last of the light glanced ruby red from a morion here, a halberd there, as the sentries paced far above.

"Run for it, lads! Once we're across the bridge they'll never take us!"

Disdaining stealth now, the band of buccaneers ran. Hairy Joes and Jake the One scooped up

Lancelot James, who cursed them for lubbers and blessed them for loyal shipmates, all in one breath. They made for the little gatehouse at the outer end of the bridge.

Six startled Spanish soldiers jumped out, like rabbits surprised on a hillside. They were met by six well-aimed pistol shots.

Yells sounded from the fortress. A gun banged off.

The shadows of rickety buildings lay ahead where the town trailed off up a hill, which was leveled and kept bare in order to give a field of fire to th fortress artillery and to afford no cover to an attacking force. The English hared down the hill, making for those shadows.

They poured into the darkness. The sky was rapidly darkening. A few stars were already out. In the darkness they would get away, steal a boat, and hey ho! for the wide Caribbean.

The sound of marching men reached them. The clink of weapons sounded. And another clinking, a mellow chiming more terrible than the sounds of weapons, a clanking and a clanging that everyone there recognized instantly.

Around the corner came a party of Spanish soldiery, led by a captain riding a white horse. The men prodded along a miserable company of prisoners. That dolorous clanking came from the chains binding the men.

Hairy Joes had said, as they reached the shadows: "We'm well away from that hellhole!"

And Bilboes Billy had answered: "That's a hothouse o' sin as I'd never wish to enter again!"

The fortress reared against the night sky at their back. The noise of the search for the escaped prisoners reached them as a confused shouting and banging. A bell was ringing.

The captain on his white horse spurred forward haughtily. He clattered across the bridge and men ran out to him. A quick conversation ensued. The prisoners were herded along, up to the gatehouse, past the six dead Spanish soldiers, and across the bridge into the fortress.

Not one of those with Shark had moved from the shadows. They should by rights be hurrying down to the waterfront to steal a boat and make their getaway. But they stayed clustered around the Captain. They watched the Spanish at the fortress, and then they swung to look at Captain Shark.

"Did you see, Cap'n?" whispered Bones.

"There was Lemuel Freeman," said Hairy Joes. "An' old Peggotty Jones, and Samivel Cropley. As well."

"Aye," said Captain Shark.

He found it difficult to breathe, almost impossible to speak. He had seen. He had seen!

"Them's our shipmates," said Lancelot James, as he hobbled up. A broom was thrust under his left elbow, and four pistols were stuck down a great red sash wound around his body. "Them's the Cap'n's men!" He shook his head. "The Cap'n!"

Shark knew Lancelot James was not speaking of Captain Sebastian Shark.

"I saw," he said, with a groan. "I saw her, Lance."

"Aye!" said the men about him, with a growling kind of savage howl, deep from their souls. "Aye, we saw her! Being taken into the fort! Captain Beth Wren! Beth Wren! Being taken down into the dungeons!"

138

# CHAPTER TWELVE

"You know what they'll do to Cap'n Beth!"

"The foul, murdering, poxed heathens!"

Shark had seen her, marching past, loaded down with chains, at the head of her crew. He had seen that bright fair hair all filthy and matted. He had seen that slender figure with the men's breeches and shirt all torn and tattered. He had not seen that glowing face with the green eyes of so much vivacity and so much scorn, eyes that could flash with complete contempt or melt into a haze of love. But he had seen Beth—Beth Wren!—being taken down to horrors he dare not contemplate for the good of his own sanity.

Shark said: "You lads have won your freedom! You c'n make it to the jetty, take a boat, be clear before morning."

Lancelot James hobbled closer, stuck his face up at Shark's. "Aye, Cap'n, reckon as how we can."

"You know what the dons will do to you if they take you up again! Well, then, what are you waiting for? Be off with you!"

"You coming, too, Cap'n?"

"I'll be along directly."

"Why ain't you a-coming along o' us now?"

This was no game they played, although they employed some of the rules of games as they talked thus, in the red-drenched shadows beneath the gaunt and frowning bulk of the fortress of San Isidro.

"I'll be along, I said! Beth Wren owes me a hatful o' pieces o' eight we took from that Spanisher *Maria Graciosa*. She laughed when she sailed off. I aim to fetch her out o' there and make her pay her just debts."

They eyed him, their filthy faces like wolves, their eyes like leeches.

"Aye, Cap'n Shark. Aye!" said Lancelot James. "Ar! An' old Lancelot James, he's the lad to help you claim your debt. Ain't that right, lads?"

"That be right, Lance," they said, in a kind of chorus.

Jan van Galen, the Dutchman, said: "You haf no chance, Captain, vidout usns." The Dutchman was right. He was a welcome addition to the force of the buccaneers. No matter what stupid wars they got up to in Europe, first one nation, then another at a third's throat, and then the second two against the first—it was all nonsense. Here in the New World there was but one enemy—or two if you counted in pirates like Bloody Fist Hagger and Goliath Niven.

"So be it, lads," said the Captain.

It was a great pity they had not managed to break out through some secret way. Some winding stair in the walls, leading through a pretty señorita's bedroom, the way of her secret lover. That would have provided them with an easy means of ingress. As it was, they had broken out through the gate and bridge over the moat. They had to find a way to break back into the evil fortress of sin and deviltry.

"Watch out, boys!" called Bones.

A party of soldiers ran swiftly from the gateway over the bridge and started off at a brisk trot down the cobbled road to the waterfront. The buccaneers hugged the shadows and watched them pass.

Two black slaves with torches came out of the gate and lit the lamps in their cressetts, one on each side of the gateway. The shadows clung more inkily in the crevices of the stonework, and moved with a deep stealthy writhing down in the moat. Presently another party of soldiers appeared, musketeers and pikemen, trotting over the bridge and down into the town. That dratted bell continued to ring.

Captain Shark stood up.

"Let us go back into that poxy den o' vipers," he said, and his voice rolled out, firm and untroubled.

Clutching their weapons, their faces as fierce and vicious as the pack of devils for whom they were named, the buccaneers followed Captain Shark across the bridge and into the fortress of San Isidro.

Isabella Castilcja's body felt on fire. Her mouth was parched. She shuddered and drew her hands up her stomach, pressing, up and up so that she cupped those firm young breasts. She squeezed so that she cried out. She stood before a mirror, clad in her shift, and she stared at herself. Her tongue crept out and licked her lips. Mother of God! What had happened to her? Why did she feel this torment?

Her uncle had arranged with the governor to provide her with an apartment in the governmental villa, for the time being, until Don Garcia returned to his estates on the other side of the island. The room was sumptuous. She had a mulatto girl to wait on her. But she did not need a girl to serve her.

She went to the door and, opening it a crack, called to the sentry at the end of the corridor.

"Tell Captain Caradonga I wish to speak to him."

"Yes, my lady," said the sentry, at once.

Isabella went back into her room. She was trembling. Presently Captain Caradonga knocked on her door and she admitted him. He wore the brave yellow and red, with a steel breastplate and a scarlet sash, and his boots were polished, and his rapier swung manfully at his hip. Isabella eyed him.

He drew himself up, staring back at her uncertainly. He licked his lips. He possessed magnificent black mustaches.

"My lady? You wished to speak to me?"

Isabella let her head roll a little to one side. She drew her stomach in. "Yes, Captain. Juan, is it not?"

At his stiff little nod, she went on: "Come, Captain, do not be so formal."

"I do not think I should be here, my lady." He gestured with one brown hand. "Your dress—"

"But, Captain Juan, it is not a dress, it is?"

Again Juan Caradonga licked his lips. He was the captain of a fine company of soldiers, although they had been decimated by the fever. They were down to a hundred and twenty now, thirty pikes and ninety shot. He valued his captaincy, did Juan Caradonga.

"Tell me, Juan. Where is Don Mercurio? I have not seen him since I returned."

"We are all delighted to see you return safely, my lady. Don Mercurio has been sent on a mission for Don Hernandez. I do not know the details. Don Hurtez slipped down the marble staircase and broke

142

his neck. So the marquis chose Don Mercurio to go instead."

"He is not here!" Isabella cried. Then she checked herself. She moved towards this handsome young captain. "Well, no matter. I am very thirsty, Captain. Would you be good enough to pour me a glass of wine?" She indicated with a graceful wave of her bare arm where the wine stood upon a low table. With stiff soldierly clumsiness Juan Caradonga poured for her and carried the wine glass across. She took it, deliberately allowing her fingers to brush his. "You had better take a glass yourself, Juan. You look tired."

He bowed and did as she bid. She turned from him and sat on the edge of the bed. Caradonga remained stiffly in the center of the room. "Oh, Juan! You big *estupido*! Come here! You are tired—this climate, the heat, the work—let me stroke your hair—"

She worked on the captain with wiles she did not know she possessed. She was aware only of the need like a hungry orchid within her belly, forcing her to do things that only Goliath Niven might have explained.

Presently she had unlatched his coat and was rubbing her palm against his chest. He swallowed and tried to draw away. Isabella drew him closer, saying: "All men desire all women, Juan. This I know! I am desirous, Juan, of knowing you!"

"But, my lady, please—"

"Hush, Juan! Let me please you." She took his hand and placed it on her breast. She could feel the tremble. She smiled and pressed herself to him. His eyes widened. Her hands moved about him, and he jerked. He could not remain the punctilious officer any longer. He threw her back upon the bed and put his hand to the hem of her shift.

Isabella laughed, deeply in her throat. She spread her legs wide and arched her back so he could draw the shift up, and she locked her arms about his neck.

This was what she craved! This, now, she could not be without, not again, ever!

"Niece!"

Don Garcia stood within the doorway. His face was flaming, and then it turned deathly pale. He leaned on his beribboned cane and his temples throbbed.

"Isabella! Captain Caradonga, you vile seducer! Rapist! Guards! Guards! I'll have you executed for this, you foul dog!"

And old Garcia hobbled across the room and began lashing Captain Caradonga about the head and shoulders with his cane.

"I did not—Don Garcia—please! For the love of God! She tempted me! She seduced me!"

"Liar! Fornicator!"

But Don Garcia saw the way Isabella lay, her posture, her lazy, indolent way of sitting up and smiling, letting her long naked legs swing down. He saw the flush on her cheeks.

"Mother of God!" he said. "Can it be true?"

Juan Caradonga knew what they would do to him. He babbled. "I swear, on my honor, señor! I swear! She asked for me, the Doña Isabella—she was dressed as you see—her shift, señor, her shift!" Caradonga fell to his knees. "I am innocent! She swore she would—the *demonios* señor—the *corsarios*! They—they—"

Don Garcia felt his body as cold as ice. He knew, at once, it was true. And yet, little Isabella? His own brother's daughter? She had seduced this stupid young fool here—yes—but why?

"Niece," said Don Garcia. "Isabella. You said the

144

*corsarios* did not harm you. You lied!"

"Oh,-no, Uncle. I did not lie. They did not harm me. I just learned things I did not know before, that is all."

"The *demonios*—they have done a thing for which there is no expiation on this earth."

Caradonga shrank back. Don Garcia looked like a carved statue of stone, engraved with lines of agony and sorrow.

The clatter of guards in the corridor heralded the arrival of five of them. Nearly all the guards were up at the fortress or chasing out after the escaped prisoners. Don Pedro was foaming and threatening to hang every mother's son of them. The guards halted at the scene. Doña Isabella covered up her naked legs. Captain Caradonga stood up. Now he was over that first blind panic. Now he could speak for his own skin.

"She said, Don Garcia, as she tempted me—" Caradonga looked away from Isabella. "She said something about needing a man, for she had not been with a man since the *demonios*—"

"Mother of God!" Don Garcia put out a hand, blindly, feeling the blood roaring and vibrating in his temples. Blood!

Blood! His honor, that honor he guarded so jealously! These gaping fools of common soldiers were standing there with their ears flapping, taking everything in. They were staring slyly at Isabella, who seemed completely unconcerned that lewd men were staring at her while she was dressed only in her undergarments. The honor of the Castilejas! Where would that honor be, in what contempt would it be held, when this story got out!

"Niece, Niece," groaned Don Garcia. "You have ruined me!"

"You, Uncle?"

Juan Caradonga said, swiftly: "The girl is not to blame if the *demonios* have led her into evil ways, señor."

"Honor!" screamed Don Garcia. "You have shamed me in the sight of the world! Slut! Wanton!"

"But, Uncle—" Isabella stood up. She still wanted a man more than anything else in the world, but her uncle was raving, and his face was as deathly pale as an alabaster statue in the cathedral. "Uncle, please—"

"Do not beg, niece! Slut! Whore! You have made me a laughing stock! You have dragged my honor in the dust! There is only one way to remove that stain upon my honor!"

Before anyone else could move, Don Garcia whipped out his rapier and, at full strength, drove the slender blade through Isabella's belly.

She stood looking uncomprehendingly down at the blade. Blood spurted just a little around the wound, staining her shift. Only a little.

Don Garcia stepped back, panting, his mouth open, spittle drooling down his chin into his beard.

"The stain is removed from the honor of the Castilejas!"

Still puzzled, Isabella put her hands to her belly. The pain was different. And there should not be any pain—only joy and giving and a great warmth and wonderful sweetness. Isabella Urraca Castileja de la Cuerva fell. She sank down as her legs gave way, and rolled onto her side. The jeweled rapier transfixed her.

"Honor!" said Don Garcia. He, too, looked without really understanding at the jeweled hilt of the rapier as it swung a little, vibrating. He looked at the steel blade thrust so forcefully through the body of his niece. "Honor," said Don Garcia. He turned, and without seeing the soldiers of Captain Juan Caradonga, he hobbled from the room.

With his left hand Captain Shark thrust the blazing torch into the Spanish captain's face. With his right toe he kicked the man betwixt wind and water. He hit him again as he went down, then he brought his rapier across and skewered a yelling soldier who was trying to brain him with a hanger.

All about him his men were belting the guards back. Pistols snapped, and in the close confines of the stone corridors the smoke hung choking like filthy gray blankets.

"On, on!" roared Captain Shark.

They were taking longer than he liked. They'd bashed their way back the way they'd come, and a few poxy guards had got in the way. Most of the soldiers were aimlessly chasing about down in the town. But they'd be back soon enough, and time was running out.

This rapier he now slid between the ribs of a soldier was the first decent one he'd come across. He withdrew and roared on. Times were a-changing and fewer and fewer soldiers wore even a breastplate. If they did—why, a cutlass to their necks was still the best way, or up between their legs like the Romans. Lancelot James, despite his urgent plea, had been left at the gate with a small mountain of pistols.

"I'll be here, Cap'n!" he'd promised. Shark did not doubt the one-eyed, one-legged buccaneer.

They roared down into the bowels of the fortress and discovered the way they had come. They met a group of jailers who fell back, flabbergasted. The buccaneers were quick with them. They pressed on.

Lorenzo, who had just about recovered from that evil kick, had made his way down to the torture chamber determined to rise to such heights of artistry in his profession that even the ice-cold Inquisitor, Father Dominic, would be pleased. And as for the fat fool, Don Pedro, he'd pay more than a miserable ducat for the stimulation he would receive. Perlita would never satisfy her hot passions with the governor if Lorenzo was not there to make a ready and purposeful assistance.

Lorenzo turned the last corner under a torch to the torture chamber—and recoiled in horror.

A mad crowd of half-naked wretches, brandishing torches and swords and pistols, flooded toward him. He turned to run. A knife flew. It smacked into Lorenzo's leather-clad back, and bit deeply. Lorenzo fell to the stone flags. He didn't understand this at all. The buccaneers poured over him, and Lorenzo would never extract information from anyone ever again—unless it was the devil himself in hell.

In the dungeons Shark gave a great booming bellow.

"Beth Wren! Cap'n Wren! Cap'n Beth!"

"I'm here, you great bellowing bull! Now hurry up and let us out, for sweet Fanny O'Brien's sake!"

"Beth! You darling!"

When they unlocked the cell she came out of it with a swaggering grace that fair mortified Shark. Even in an old shirt and breeches, with her fair hair wildly disarranged, her face smudged and filthy, and matted blood clotted down her cheek, she looked gorgeously lovely in Shark's eyes. Truth to tell, any man would have found her gorgeous. Many a man had tried to prove that, in ways that Beth Wren had disapproved of, and so many a man had felt a rapier between his ribs or a pistol ball in his guts.

"What're you gawping at, Sebastian?"

"Nothing, Beth."

"Well, if that's the best you can do at nothing, how in tarnation are we goin' to git out of here, hey, me bully boy?"

"Come on," shouted Bones. He looked leaner and grimmer than ever, and part of his white hair had been singed off. That was when a Spaniard had tried to smash away the torch thrust into his eyes. "We ain't got all night."

"After you, Beth," said Shark, and he bowed in the exquisite way of the Restoration fop.

"Ar, Sebastian, me darling! If only you was a real gent!"

"But I'm not, Beth, and for that you give thanks to your patron saint."

"Now don't start gitting papist, Cap'n!"

They guffawed at this and then turned in a body ready to fight their way out of this stinking hell hole.

Strangely enough, getting out proved easier than breaking in. Shark knew that would not last. They had disposed of soldiers on the way in, and the fortress had been denuded of the rest to search along the waterfront. Pretty soon this fresh fracas at the fort would bring the soldiers hurrying back. Before they reached the gate and bridge, where Lancelot James waited with his pistols in a ranked heap, the buccaneers must be out of here.

As it happened, as Lancelot James told them with much feeling, they got there just in time to stop the fun.

James was sitting with his back propped comfortably against the side wall, under a flaring lantern with a broken light. That uncertain light cast a deep shadow directly beneath it, where Lancelot sat, and gave sufficient illumination for him to pick his targets. As Shark stepped through the gateway, James's pistol belched and a Spaniard, trying to run forward over the bridge, screeched and jackknifed. Another followed on his heels, and James snatched up another pistol and shot him fairly in the breast bone. Both men pitched sideways and toppled into the moat.

"Fair shooting, Lance." said the Captain.

"Fair! Shiver me timbers, Cap'n! It's like a little targit practiss, surely it is!" He picked up another pistol. "I've seven left, Cap'n. Cain't old Lance James have seven more shots? Just for luck, like?"

"No, old Lance James cannot," said Shark, firmly. Hairy Joes and Jake the One stepped forward and hoisted Lancelot James. He screeched at them.

"I've me broomstick! Leggo, you lubbers!"

But they took him up and they all ran out over the bridge. A musket cracked from the ramparts and Oswald staggered.

"Grab Oswald!" bellowed Shark.

Johnny Chance, his mouth open now and yelling defiance, grabbed Oswald. Oswald was a huge Negro, a splendid man, and no one wished to lose him. Together, Johnny Chance and Oswald ran with the others into the shadows.

Now, Captain Sebastian Shark had to make a decision.

He had noticed that many of the men were looking naturally to Beth Wren for orders. She was their captain. She had a brace of pistols stuck down the sash wound around her waist. Her figure permitted of few more. She waved a rapier. She knew how to use it, too.

"Beth," said Shark, urgently. "We can't get down to the waterfront yet. They'll be thicker than fleas in a Spaniard's blanket down there."

"I know, Sebastian. We'll have to make inland. Get into th' hills. They'll never find us there."

Shark didn't like this; but it seemed the obvious course.

Bones said, low: "More soldiers, Cap'n."

Everyone hunkered down in the shadows, scarcely breathing, until the Spaniards had trotted past, going up toward the bridge and gate.

"We'll likely starve or die o' thirst in the hills, Beth. And we'll have to come out one day, when they're still ready for us, knowing we're up there."

"Well?"

"They're pulling back, coming up here to see what the disturbance is. If we sneak down, nice and quiet like, they'll most likely be few enough of 'em left on the waterfront."

Beth Wren was not one to argue. Shark knew that if she said she would go into the hills, she'd go, by God. And, what's more, she'd take well over half of the men with her.

She stared at him, her head on one side, her hands on her hips. She looked wonderful.

"All right, Sebastian. We'll go down to the waterfront. But if we're caught, I'll spit on your grave, so help me!"

"I'll drink to that, Beth."

They stalked through the night. They kept low and avoided the soldiers, and so came undetected to the waterfront.

Out there, with their great stern lanterns blazing, lay Don Hernandez's three ships. A fourth lay a little way off, and, alongside her, chained up, lay *Robin's Blood*, Captain Wren's bark. Shark stared toward the ships, calculating. What a coup it would be to cut out that great *Nuestra Señora del Rosario*! But she was so anchored that the other two ships blocked her swift passage to the open sea. They, in their turn, were anchored awkwardly for a rapid departure. As for the ship that had brought in *Robin's Blood*, Beth said that she was in a sorry state, for the battle had been bloody and nasty, and *Robin's Blood* had been taken by a stratagem. She didn't want to talk about it. Buccaneers had a pride when it came to their ships.

What a stroke, though, to make off with the flagship of this Spanish squadron!

Shark sighed. It couldn't be done. Oh, yes, he could do it; but there was not the time. Long before they had her clear, every other ship in the harbor would be able to pour broadside after broadside into her. Even then, they might win through. But they would suffer. Many good men would be killed—and for what? Just so he could boast he had taken the Spanish flagship?

Of course he could justify his decision if he did decide to take the flagship. The world might say he was wrong. But it was in the nature of a man to say the world was wrong and he was right in justification of his acts. Shark had seen captains go that way, monsters of self-esteem, preening themselves on their own prowess, never wrong. No, by God! He swung back to his pack of desperadoes, his face long and grim in determination, and Beth Wren said:

"That tarnation great flagship, Sebastian! That'll do us! We'll cut her out and sail away and spit in th' dons' faces! Sink me else!"

Shark kept his temper down. He sighed. "Then

it's sunk you'll be, my darling. See the way she's anchored up—aye, and they've moored her, too. By the time we would be free o' those two others, we'd be burning from truck to keelson."

She stared up at him, her hands on her hips, her head flung back. He saw the deviltry in those green eyes. He saw that luscious rosebud mouth firming from its delectable pout into the gash of a shrew.

"What's this, Cap'n Shark? Standin' back from taking a Spanisher! My oath, Sebastian, what ails you, lad?"

"You'd kill three quarters of your own men!"

"Never!" she swung about violently to appeal to her crew.

Lancelot James said: "Ar! Old Lancelot James knows! Cap'n Beth, Cap'n Beth—this time and by a miracle, on my oath, Cap'n Shark be in the right o' it."

"You, too, Lancelot!"

"I know a handful of determined men can perform miracles against the dons," said Shark. "I know. I marched with Harry Morgan and I saw. But not this time."

"Well then, Sebastian," she said with a scornful voice that cut him. "What should we do? Give ourselves up?"

Bones said: "We could attempt *Robin's Blood*. She's lying outside th' others."

"Aye!" said Cap'n Beth. "Aye! I'll fight to take back me own ship!"

"No," said Captain Shark.

She drew an astonished breath.

She was about to break into an impassioned tirade when Johnny Chance whispered in a breath like whetted steel: "Quiet! The Spanish dogs are a-prowling agin!"

They waited quietly. Beth Wren crouched by

Shark. He put a hand around her waist and pressed. After a time she lifted that powerful hand and put it more comfortably upon her breast. Shark squeezed her. They exchanged no words. Words were unnecessary.

When the patrol of soldiers looking for them had gone, they emerged from the shadows.

"You said no, Sebastian!"

"Aye, Beth, I said no. *Robin's Blood* won't do. You said the don who took you was shot up, so your pickle boat is, too."

"I'd like to take your tail and stuff it—"

Some of the buccaneers chuckled at this. They were a cutthroat crew. They all knew that their present dilemma could end all wrong. By this time tomorrow night they could be screaming their guts out on the rack, or having their legs crushed, or boiling oil could be pouring down their mouths. They lived a harsh and unlovely life, and they took what they could of life and reckoned it cheap. Captain Shark alone valued life at more than a pot of gold and a pot of rum.

"We'll take that little sloop riding out there, Beth. We can swim out, and them as can't swim will have to wait for a boat. Lance can look after them."

"Aye, Cap'n," said James. "I still have seven shots left."

"You're sure, Sebastian?" Beth sounded wistful.

"Sure."

"Well, promise me on your word we'll take that great flagship, one day soon!"

Shark did not laugh. He said: "I don't give my word, for it is worth nothing. I will never keep a promise if it don't suit me book."

154

"I know that, you great lummox! But it's me, Cap'n Beth, who's asking!"

He put both his hands on her shoulders. There was light enough for him to see the reflected glitter in those green eyes. "I'll promise you, Beth, if it pleases you. But don't count on it."

"You great poxy gallantifangasting pirate! Why, I'll—"

Shark lifted Captain Beth Wren under the armpits and hoisted her high. They walked to the edge of the jetty, the cap'n and Beth's crew, they slid into the water like eels, and Lancelot James and the nonswimmers watched them go. Soon a boat would be back for them.

"Ar!" said Lancelot James, to no one in particular. "Old Lancelot James knows what's what. Cap'n Shark wants to make sure o' that hatful o' pieces o' eight Cap'n Beth owes him from *Maria Graciosa*."

"When will they come back for us?" said one of the non-swimmers. He sounded fretful.

"Don't get breezy," said Lancelot James. "If Cap'n Shark says he'll be back, he'll be back, mark me, lad! Oh, yes, Cap'n Shark will return!"

# GLOSSARY

**articles**: agreement drawn up by pirate ship's company stipulating proportions of shares in plunder, compensation for loss of limbs, etc., and regulating other areas of possible conflict. Based on privateer articles.

**bagnio**: a prison where slaves are kept.

**baldric**: a leather belt worn across the chest and over one shoulder, used to support a cutlass.

**bilboes**: two iron bars with sliding shackles to fix a prisoner by his legs in a sitting position.

**breaker**: a small cask of water carried by a ship's lifeboat.

**buccaneer**: from the Carib word *bukan*, a grill for drying meat. The French called the meat *viande boucanée*, and the hunters who caught and grilled the meat *boucanier*. Only the English called the sea rovers buccaneers.

**cannon**: at this time a gun of about 8,000 pounds in weight and of about eight inches caliber, firing a shot weighing 58 lbs.

**converso**: Spanish word for a convert, one who has joined the Catholic faith.

**corsarios luteranos**: Lutheran corsairs, Spanish name for buccaneers.

**cresset:** a portable torch, made by burning oil in a small metal cup.

**culverin:** or culvering, a gun of about 4,500 lbs in the ordinary size, caliber 5.25", weight of shot 17.31 lbs.

**demiculverin:** a gun of about 2,700 lbs in the ordinary size, caliber 4.5", weight of shot 10.26 lbs.

**ducat:** gold coin, first struck by the dukes of Apulia in the twelfth century; the word "ducatus" in the inscription gave the coin its name.

**falcon:** or faulcon or faucon, a gun of about 750 lbs, caliber 2.75", and weight of shot 2.5 lbs.

**filibustiers:** French name for buccaneers.

**halberd:** a weapon, consisting of a battle-ax and spike on a long pole.

**hanger:** a short sword, popular with seamen.

**harquebus:** a heavy matchlock gun, usually fired from a support.

**hawsehole:** a hole in a ship's bow through which a cable is passed.

**hidalgo:** Spanish gentleman.

**hijo de puta:** son of a doxy.

**ladrón:** Spanish word for thief.

**leech:** one who performs a doctor's duties aboard a ship.

**letters of marque and reprisal:** a letter patent authorizing a privateer to seize foreign goods; much abused in use.

**lobos marinos:** sea wolves.

**orlop:** the lowest deck of a ship.

**peruke:** a curly, elaborate wig worn by gentlemen.

**piece of eight:** Spanish silver coin, worth eight Spanish reals.

**pinnace:** a ship's lifeboat.

**privateer:** loosely, as in Captain Shark's case, a privately owned vessel which volunteers to wage war against a particular foreign enemy.

**rabato:** lace neckcloth coming historically between the ruff and the cravat. A form of falling collar.

**saker:** a gun of about 1,500 lbs. weight in the ordinary size, a caliber of 3.75", weight of shot 6 lbs.

**tampions:** plugs in the mouths of cannons or heavy guns, necessary to keep the muzzles clean between firings.

**zee-rovers:** Dutch word for buccaneers.

The fascinating story behind
the greatest naval adventures of all time.
the saga of Horatio Hornblower

425 440 $1.95

# The Hornblower Companion

## C. S. FORESTER

· The complete and indispensable guide.
Fully illustrated with maps, charts, and drawings
by Samuel H. Bryant

---

**P440    THE HORNBLOWER COMPANION        $1.95**

**TO ORDER**

Please check the space next to the book/s you want, send this order
form together with your check or money order, include the price of
the book/s and 25¢ for handling and mailing to:

**PINNACLE BOOKS, INC. / P.O. Box 4347**
**Grand Central Station / New York, N.Y. 10017**

☐ **CHECK HERE IF YOU WANT A FREE CATALOG**

I have enclosed $＿＿＿＿check＿＿＿＿＿＿or money order＿＿＿＿
as payment in full. No C.O.D.'s

Name＿＿＿＿＿＿＿＿＿＿＿＿＿＿＿＿＿＿＿＿＿＿＿＿＿＿＿

Address＿＿＿＿＿＿＿＿＿＿＿＿＿＿＿＿＿＿＿＿＿＿＿＿＿

City＿＿＿＿＿＿＿＿＿＿＿State＿＿＿＿＿Zip＿＿＿＿＿＿
(Please allow time for delivery)

**THE INCREDIBLE ACTION PACKED SERIES**

# DEATH MERCHANT

### by Joseph Rosenberger

His name is Richard Camellion, he's a master of disguise, deception and destruction. He does what the CIA and FBI cannot do. They call him THE DEATH MERCHANT!

| Order | | Title | Book # | Price |
|---|---|---|---|---|
| _____ | # 1 | THE DEATH MERCHANT | P0211 | .95 |
| _____ | # 2 | OPERATION OVERKILL | P245 | .95 |
| _____ | # 3 | THE PSYCHOTRAN PLOT | P117 | .95 |
| _____ | # 4 | CHINESE CONSPIRACY | P168 | .95 |
| _____ | # 5 | SATAN STRIKE | P182 | .95 |
| _____ | # 6 | ALBANIAN CONNECTION | P670 | 1.25 |
| _____ | # 7 | CASTRO FILE | P264 | .95 |
| _____ | # 8 | BILLIONAIRE MISSION | P339 | .95 |
| _____ | # 9 | THE LASER WAR | P399 | .95 |
| _____ | #10 | THE MAINLINE PLOT | P473 | 1.25 |
| _____ | #11 | MANHATTAN WIPEOUT | P561 | 1.25 |

AND MORE TO COME . . .

**TO ORDER**

Please check the space next to the book/s you want, send this order form together with your check or money order, include the price of the book/s and 25¢ for handling and mailing to:

PINNACLE BOOKS, INC. / P.O. Box 4347
Grand Central Station / New York, N.Y. 10017

☐ CHECK HERE IF YOU WANT A FREE CATALOG

I have enclosed $_____ check_____ or money order_____
as payment in full. No C.O.D.'s

Name_____

Address_____

City_____State_____Zip_____
Please allow time for delivery)

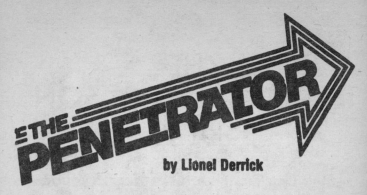

# THE PENETRATOR

### by Lionel Derrick

Mark Hardin. Discharged from the army, after service in Vietnam. His military career was over. But *his* war was just beginning. His reason for living and reason for dying become the same—to stamp out crime and corruption wherever he finds it. He is deadly; he is unpredictable; and he is dedicated. He is The Penetrator!

Read all of him in:

| Order | | Title | Book # | Price |
|---|---|---|---|---|
| _____ | # 1 | THE TARGET IS H | P236 | .95¢ |
| _____ | # 2 | BLOOD ON THE STRIP | P237 | .95¢ |
| _____ | # 3 | CAPITOL HELL | P318 | .95¢ |
| _____ | # 4 | HIJACKING MANHATTAN | P338 | .95¢ |
| _____ | # 5 | MARDI GRAS MASSACRE | P378 | .95¢ |
| _____ | # 6 | TOKYO PURPLE | P434 | $1.25 |
| _____ | # 7 | BAJA BANDIDOS | P502 | $1.25 |
| _____ | # 8 | THE NORTHWEST CONTRACT | P540 | $1.25 |

**TO ORDER**                                        AND MORE TO COME . . .

Please check the space next to the book/s you want, send this order form together with your check or money order, include the price of the book/s and 25¢ for handling and mailing to:

**PINNACLE BOOKS, INC. / P.O. Box 4347**
**Grand Central Station / New York, N.Y. 10017**

☐ **CHECK HERE IF YOU WANT A FREE CATALOG**

I have enclosed $_____ check_____ or money order_____ as payment in full. No C.O.D.'s

Name_____

Address_____

City_____ State_____ Zip_____
(Please allow time for delivery)

# A THRILLING
# SUSPENSE TRILOGY
# by CLIVE EGLETON

"... these Egleton books are among the best of their type."
—*The San Francisco Chronicle*

Russia has devastated Britain with a nuclear attack and is occupying the country. The English people unite against this oppression and form an underground resistance network to fight for their freedom against seemingly overwhelming odds.

## LAST POST FOR A PARTISAN

Five years after the holocaust a split in England's resistance is jeopardizing the entire movement. David Garnett is called in to find and eliminate the traitors in a deadly game of violence and intrigue in which everyone is suspect.

P344    $1.25

## A PIECE OF RESISTANCE

It is the near future and England has been conquered and occupied by the Soviets. When the assassin of a high Russian official is captured and sent to a maximum-security prison, the underground resistance plots an incredible mission to rescue the assassin.    P315    $1.25

## THE JUDAS MANDATE

In the final novel of this electrifying trilogy, David Garnett must carry out his riskiest assignment yet, involving the release of political prisoners who will try to form a government in exile in the United States.    P352    $1.25